Angels

Angels

DENIS JOHNSON

Alfred A. Knopf   New York   1983

Library of Congress Cataloging in Publication Data
Johnson, Denis. [date] Angels.
I. Title.
PS3560.03745A63   1983   813'.54   83-47782
ISBN 0-394-53225-2

*this book is dedicated to H. P.
and to those who have shared
their experience, strength, and hope*

I accused her as though her prayers had really
worked the change:
    What did I do to you that you had to condemn
me to life?

GRAHAM GREENE
The End of the Affair

Angels

1

In the Oakland Greyhound all the people were dwarfs, and they pushed and shoved to get on the bus, even cutting in ahead of the two nuns, who were there first. The two nuns smiled sweetly at Miranda and Baby Ellen and played I-see-you behind their fingers when they'd taken their seats. But Jamie could sense that they found her make-up too thick, her pants too tight. They knew she was leaving her husband, and figured she'd turn for a living to whoring. She wanted to tell them what was what, but you can't talk to a Catholic. The shorter nun carried a bright cut rose wrapped in her two hands.

Jamie sat by the window looking out and smoking a Kool. People still crowded at the bus's door, people she hoped never to meet—struggling with mutilated luggage and paper sacks that might have contained, the way they handled them, the reasons for their every regretted act and the justifications for their wounds. A black man in a tweed suit and straw hat held up a sign for his departing relatives: "THE SUN SHALL BE TURNED INTO DARKNESS AND THE MOON INTO BLOOD" (JOEL 2:31). Under the circumstances, Jamie felt close to this stranger.

Around three in the morning Jamie's eyes came open. Headlights on an entrance ramp cut across their flight and swept through the bus, and momentarily in her exhaustion she thought it was the flaming head of a man whipping like a comet through the sleeping darkness of these travellers, hers alone to witness. Suddenly Miranda was awake, jabbering in her ear, excited to be up past bedtime.

Jamie pushed the child's words away, afraid of the dark the bus was rushing into, confused at being swallowed up so quickly by her new life, fearful she'd be digested in a flash and spit out the other end in the form of an old lady too dizzy to wonder where her youth had gone. A couple of times she tried to shush Miranda, because the baby was sleeping and so was everyone else on the bus, except the driver, she hoped—but Miranda had to nudge Baby Ellen with her foot every two seconds because she wanted to play, right in the middle of Nevada in the middle of the night. "Randy," Jamie said. "I'm tarred now, hon. Don't wake up Ellen now."

Miranda sat on her hands and pretended to sleep, secretly nudging Baby Ellen with her foot.

"Move your foot, hon," Jamie told her. "I ain't playing. Move your foot now."

Miranda feigned sleep and deafness, her foot jerking in a dream to jostle the baby.

"Move—yer—*fut*," Jamie whispered fiercely, and grabbed her ankle and moved it. "You behave. Or I'll tell the driver, and he'll take you and put you off the bus, right out there in that desert. Right in the dark, with the snakes. You hear me?" She jerked

Miranda's foot away again. "Don't you play like you're asleep when I can see goddamn it you ain't!"

She stared with hatred at Miranda's closed eyes and soon realized the child had fallen asleep. The weightlessness of fear replaced the weight of anger as the bus sailed down the gullet the headlights made. She put her hand over her face and wept.

In a little while she fell asleep, and dreamed about a man drowning in a cloud of poison. She woke up and wondered if this was a dream about her husband, or what?—a dream about the past, or a dream about the future?

Baby Ellen wouldn't stop screaming.

Jamie held her in one arm, searching beneath the seat with her free hand for the travelling bag, then in the travelling bag for Baby Ellen's orange juice. "There there there there there," she told Baby Ellen. "Have a crib for you soon, and a string to tie on your music box with, and Mama and Miranda'll come sing to you when it's bedtime, and here's your orange juice, thank goodness, there there there there there, little Baby Ellen, oh that a *good* orange juice, such a *serious* orange juice, such a *serious* look, oh, see the pretty sun? See the sun over there, Baby Ellen? That's just a little bitty part of the sun, pretty soon Baby Ellen see the whole sun and then it's morning time for Baby Ellen and Mama and Miranda Sue." She wished she could smother the baby. Nobody would know. They were four days out of Oakland.

She fed Baby Ellen her orange juice and watched the sun as it moved into prominence above the dead cornfields in Indiana, the light striking her face painfully as it ticked over the frozen pools and the rows of broken stalks glazed with ice. Her husband angrily sold stereophonic components for a living. He brooded on his life, and it grew on him until he was rattling around inside of it. Why couldn't she just be thankful to him, he always wanted to know, since he was losing track of what *he* wanted just so *she* could have everything *she* wanted? Couldn't she see how everything kept happening? It was just—he pounded his fist on the wall so the small trailer shook—*one moment goes to the next . . .* He choked her close to death twice, frantic to think she couldn't understand his complaint. And she couldn't. He slept almost every minute he was at home. At night, he cried and confessed how everything scared him. Whenever she looked at him he had his face in his arms, hiding from the pictures in his own brain. Finally he'd blown it, their whole marriage. She'd seen it coming like a red caboose at the end of a train.

Cut loose between Oakland and everything that would happen next, she couldn't stand to let the bus keep moving and thought, I'll get off this bus at the breakfast stop and change my ticket for the next bus on home, and happy trails, all you folks in Greyhound-land. He'd be overjoyed to see her, she was certain of it. What would she say? Forgot my toothbrush, she told herself, and smiled. Forgot my purse. Left my lunch behind. The ticket man would laugh in her face for turning around right in the middle. Liked the trip so much, you thought you'd start all over, said the ticket man. Yeah, have to go back and look out the left side this time, in case I missed something special. At the breakfast stop, Jamie paid a lady to look after Miranda and Baby Ellen while she took a sponge bath in the ladies' room. Miranda stood on a tomato soup crate to play the pinball and took pictures of herself holding her baby sister in a little booth with a curtain. Jamie and Miranda ate cornflakes, and Baby Ellen had apricot-peach dessert. They were running out of money. The turnpike took on more curves and hills as it came toward Cleveland.

Three seats back and on the other side of the aisle, the two nuns sat muttering to themselves, sleepy with breakfast. Secretly Jamie watched, and she realized they were praying, the bright cut rose the shorter nun had been clutching in Oakland now replaced by a dark rosary. Jamie wondered if they made nuns pray each day after breakfast. Did they think to themselves, here I go, praying, and did they hold a portrait in their heads of God's face with his white beard, nodding thoughtfully at their Latin? If praying was their job, then did they get any holidays? She glanced at Miranda making broad, even strokes with a crayon across a woman's face in *People* magazine, and wondered if her own little girl would ever be a nun with a black and white hat on top of her long hair. But then, Miranda wasn't a Catholic. They hadn't been much of anything in Oakland, though they'd been retired Baptists in West Virginia before the move. You couldn't be very burning for your religion in California, because California was full of atheists and Birchers and Hare Krishnas, and the only ones very serious about religion were the crazy people like that, who were always jumping off the Golden Gate when seized by the power of God. Baptism seemed just another way of getting yourself wet.

In California there were funny-eyed old women convinced the world would momentarily come to an end, or that spacemen would be landing soon for the Judgment. You picked Venusians or Martians or Jesus Christ, or people with twelve arms and blue skin from India. Sodom and Gomorrah had been destroyed by an atom bomb dropped from a rocket ship.

Jamie heard low snores issuing from the shorter nun when she was supposed to be praying. God had heard it all before anyway, and didn't bother to wake her. From nowhere the bright rose had appeared again, and she choked it in her two hands while she slept.

The man in the seat behind them, Jamie could tell, had her figured for some kind of thrill-seeker. But he was a nice man with a kindly grin and a tattoo of a seahorse on his left arm that fascinated Miranda. "King Neptune gave it to me," he told her, and winked at Jamie and rolled his coatsleeve back down, and that was all he'd say about his tattoo.

As the morning passed, Miranda drew him into her activities, and by the afternoon they were terrific buddies. In his airline bag he had four beers, and offered one to Jamie. For all the pushing and shoving and disrespect for nuns shown on this trip, the seat beside him, as were several others, was vacant. She accepted his invitation to join him. "Thought you were about to jump clear off this bus a while ago," he said. "I think your kids are drilling your head a little bit." He was wearing his glasses now—silvered wrap-around sunshades—so that he had two mirrors instead of eyes. In his face she saw her own face.

And he sported a pencil-thin mustache that just made her ill. A little bit of foam clung to it briefly, and then he licked it away. "I don't never take no planes," he said. "I get sick as a dog on one, even on a cross-the-country jet. I was hitching, but I started to freeze." He jiggled his beer can, popping its aluminum rapidly in his grip. "So now I'm taking the bus. Which I guess you can see for yourself," he said.

"Half the time I can't see anything for myself." She gestured with her Stroh's toward the seat in front of them, where Miranda and Baby Ellen both napped. "Like to drive anybody half blind, looking after them two twenty-four hours ever day." Stroh's, she noticed, was Shorts written backwards. She had never heard of this beer.

"Going to Pittsburgh for some high old times," the man said. "I got me some bread, but I ain't spending none except on wine, women, and song. So that's why I was hitching."

"Jesus," Jamie said. "Twenty-four hours a day ever single day of the year."

"Yeah. Yeah, I guess so," said the man.

"Till Miranda's eighteen, and then Ellen'll be—what, twelve? No, eighteen take away five, that's thirteen she'll be. Then five more years till Ellen's grown up, and that makes twenty-three years in all."

"That's a big job you got," the man said.

"No fooling. And then when you're done you're a dried-up old sack and when somebody says What you been doing all these years, you got no idea what in the world to say. Just like a hermit. Just like a nun."

"You better take you a night off next Sairdy," the man said.

She wondered what he was getting around to, and looked right at him. He was about forty, maybe a bit younger. He had curly hair not yet actually too thin, but preparing to go bald in the front. Under a western-style suit coat, designed apparently for a cowboy bandleader, he wore a white teeshirt. He removed the coat now, holding his can of beer between his knees as he did so, and uncovered the shirt's emblem: "Harrah's—Vegas." When he poked his wraparound sunglasses back onto the bridge of his nose with his thumb, his shirtsleeve rose with the movement to reveal a tattoo on his triceps of a single naked breast cupped in two disembodied hands. "Let me guess. I bet your name is Louise," he said.

"No way. My name's Jamie." She looked in the rear-vision mirror, trying to see the driver, wondering if he'd noticed the obscene tattoo on the upper arm of the man she was suddenly sharing a seat with. She could only see the driver's ear in the mirror, she thought, and maybe part of his cap.

"You nervous about that driver? He don't see a thing, Jamie." The man gulped from his beer without ducking to conceal the action. "He don't see."

"How do you know? Where'd you get all this information?"

"I been a driver before. All's you can see is if somebody's in a seat or out of it. And only some of the seats. You got no way of telling if they're drinking beer or pop, or if they're asleep or awake or what they're doing."

They observed the power lines as they dipped and swooped and ran by over the phone poles, the straight rows in the planted fields, less occasional now in Ohio, as they spread out like fans from the horizon, then whipped shut as they passed. The sky had gone grey after dawn, and the hills pushed up directly against the burden of it; a few winter birds glided and wheeled just under it. "Let the boy rock and roll," she hummed to herself, and the man hummed a melody too, interjecting a hissy whistle into the tune.

"Nope. Nope. No sir," the man said, popping his beer can. She glanced at him, but he didn't continue, and she turned her eyes again to the fields running away beside them. "Nope, Jamie, nobody sees this," he said suddenly, and kissed her cheek.

She swallowed beer. "Hey now—quit!"

"Quit what?"

"I'm married!"

"Where's your husband?"

"He's home."

"Where's that?"

"He's home. He's at the next stop. He's in Cincinnati."

"This bus don't go to Cincinnati."

"He'll meet us in Cleveland then."

"Now, I heard you telling your little girl a while back, she won't see Daddy no more." He grinned and opened another beer. It hissed loudly opening and she jerked. No one had noticed. The two nuns were asleep toward the back, one leaning against the windowpane and the other resting her head on her shoulder.

"Well," Jamie said, "I had to leave him."

"Now we're getting honest."

"Honesty is the best policy."

"Have another beer, before I drink it all up."

"You didn't even say your name yet."

"Name's Bill. Bill Houston. Told it to your little girl there, and I thought you must've heard." He took her hand in his.

"Hey, I can't use this," she said. "Specially at this moment. Why don't you just get straight?"

"Oh, all right," he said. "Forget it. Hey—here. I got something here going to make that beer taste like champagne." He sneaked a pint bottle of bourbon from his bag, and, catching hold of her wrist, he sloshed some into her can of beer. "That'll perk her up. Called a Depth Charger." He slapped his nose with a forefinger, rolling his eyes and allowing his tongue to fall from the corner of his mouth. A little stupid, but Jamie couldn't help laughing.

She sipped from her drink and they discussed the passage of eras, the transformation of the landscape, the confusion of people in high places, the impersonality of the interstates. The bus carried them out from under the cloudbank covering Western Ohio into a rarefied light where old patches of snow burned fiercely in the dirt of hillsides. Soon the beer was gone and the cans held only bourbon. "You don't have to be afraid of me," Bill Houston said. "I been married three times."

"Three times? What for?" she said.

"I never could figure out what for myself. After the first time I said, next time you want to do something like that, you better remember. So I got this here." He displayed a tattoo on the inside of his elbow, a tiny feminine Satan's face over the motto, Remember Annie. "Didn't do me no good. Three months later I was right back married again, to a big and fat one. First one, she was little and skinny, so the next one I made sure she was big and fat, sort of for the variety."

"Variety's important."

"Yes it is. Variety's important."

"Course, you have to be dependable, too."

"Third one I married was dependable. I could just never get my mind around it—she was so dependable, but then one day right in the middle of everything she says, what was your first wife's name. I says it was Annie; she says, oh yeah, Annie what, and I says, Annie Klein! What you asking me for? Well, she was just wondering. So about five minutes later she wants to know what was my next wife's name. So course I told her, which it happened to be the same maiden name as *she* had. That why you picked me? she wants to know. What do you mean, I told her, coming up on me all of a sudden with this shit—excuse me. She says, so, I'm wife number three, and Roberts number two, but when it comes to number one, honey, I ain't nothing, and next day she filed. Just all of a sudden like that. I says hey! you're number one! you're number one! But she just went on ahead and filed. Very weird lady."

Jamie said, "You in a band someplace?"

"Me? In a music band, you mean?" He took a pull of his beer, and Jamie fingered the shiny material of his jacket on the seat between them.

"Truth is, I got it at a second-hand type thrift shop," he said. "I must've been under the weather or something. Anyway, what the hell. It don't fit too bad. You know any jokes?"

"Jokes," Jamie said, trying out the word as if for the first time ever.

"Yeah, you know. Like ho ho ho."

"Right," Jamie said.

A spell of dizziness stabbed her head and then passed away. She sensed how the dead smoke of ten thousand cigarets caked the air. Out there in the blinding day the winter would sting your lungs, but here they carried with them a perpetual stifled twilight and a private exhaustion. She didn't know if she was coming awake or going crazy.

And Bill Houston said, "How come they ran out of ice cubes in Poland?"

"This a joke now?" she said.

He was irritated. *"Yeah."*

"Okay—how come they ran out of ice cubes in Poland?"

"Wait a minute. Wait a minute. Are you asking me?"

"I must be. Because I sure as hell don't know the answer. You know what we need?" she said. "Ice cubes." She had a feeling she might be laughing a little too loudly.

"Hey, I'm really getting off on this whole conversation," he said with fervor. Good-fellowship thickened his voice. "Now listen: how come there's no ice cubes in Poland?"

"Because they ran out. We just went through all that."

He shook his head. "I can see you're a hard one to deal with," he said with some respect.

"No, I'm not, really." She let her gaze drift out into Ohio. Her mood went blank. "It's just that I'm going to be into some of that divorce stuff pretty soon myself."

"Don't let it get to you. You just stand there, and everything they say, you say yes. Pretty soon you'll be divorced. It don't feel no different."

"I think it might probably feel different," she said.

"I don't know," he said. "Never felt a bit different to me. Course, pretty soon, being married was the difference, and getting divorced was the usual."

"That ain't going to be my way. I'm single from here on out."

"You just keep saying that, like I did."

"You just watch. Once is enough, brother. I had a man running around on me once—that's all, that's it. Not no more. Thanks anyway."

"Well. Takes a lot of will power, stick to the same brand all the time with no variety."

"I stuck to the same brand! Wasn't no trouble to *me!* He only had to stay out three nights, and I said that's that. Three nights is just about three nights too many, I says to him. Wasn't long before I found out who it was, and how many times, and ever-

thing. I told him, I'm hard to fool. And I am. Hey." She stared minutely forward, scrutinizing the nearer distances. "Do I look like I'm loaded?"

Bill Houston said he'd been working some place for the last few months, but she didn't believe it. He'd had something to do with oil rigging, she wasn't paying much attention. He'd saved up some money, perhaps a good deal of money, and he was lonesome. Cleveland went by like a collection of billboards.

Without actually deciding yes or no, she found she'd agreed to stay over a day in Pittsburgh and see the town with Bill Houston before travelling on to Hershey, where she intended to take up residence with her sister-in-law. But didn't Hershey come before Pittsburgh? Or didn't the place where they were supposed to change for Hershey come first? He didn't know. She didn't know, either, and by God she didn't care. She'd been on this bus five days and couldn't care less. Let her sister-in-law wait all day and all night at the bus station—let Hershey, Pennsylvania, wait one more day for her; she'd been waiting five days for Hershey, Pennsylvania.

She'd discussed killing herself, she confessed, with Sarah Miller, her best friend, who'd gone to the same high school in West Virginia. Discussed how she'd do it in the style of Marilyn Monroe. She'd clean the trailer completely, and dress up in her black negligee. She'd use Sarah's ex-husband's revolver, and Sarah would listen in the night for the shot, and then listen in case the kids woke up. She'd stand right in the doorway when she did it, so she'd be the first thing he found when he came home late from running around on her, stretched out on the floor like a dark Raggedy Ann doll with her brains in the kitchen. Because already he'd stayed out two nights in a row. That was that, that was all, so long. The note would go like this: No Thanks.

But you know who he was doing it with, Bill? Want to know who? Sarah. Old Sarah from the same high school six years ago, same graduation, same California trailer village, and now same lover, same everything, Sarah Miller. Because on the third night, she couldn't take this treatment, not for one second more. She snuck over to Sarah's to borrow the gun and there he was, sneaking home, out of Sarah's trailer with the door creaking so loud in the quiet she took it for herself, screeching, Bill, and he saw, and she saw, and Sarah in the doorway with her panties saw, so everyone knew that everyone else knew what was what with who. If anybody knows how to handle that kind of a scene, they can tell the world on Johnny Carson or whatever and make a million. So she left. What could anybody say? Just had to pack and not look at each other and be very very quiet, even though Sarah came and was going to knock on the door but went away before she could make herself, twice; and then at nine-thirty the Yellow Cab for the Greyhound and the new life; and she'd left him standing in the kitchen with half a grapefruit in his hand. Everyone was observing her as she wept on Bill Houston's obscenely glamorized shoulder.

She went to the toilet in the back to be sick. Briefly she tried to be graceful, and then she blundered from one pair of seats to the next, commenting angrily on the erratic and inconsiderate driving around here. Wasn't that the way? Never a bus driver who knows where the road even *is*. Three feet from the door she declared she'd changed her mind and would be sick wherever she felt like it, and watch out because she probably would, any second now. Right now she'd see if she wanted to walk a bit more, or be sick first. She'd walk up and down the aisle here for a minute, to take the air and cry for a minute.

And goddamn it, didn't she have a right to cry with the kids driving her crazy for five days on a bus with the windows going by like a movie? You can give her permission to cry or just go on back to your convent with your rose in your teeth. I'll puke here if I want to or anywhere I want to, Sugar. Keep smiling but I can see what you think, the goddamn white line goes right through me every time I close my eyes five days on this bus. Go on, smile. I can see you got to make yourself smile and smile with your convent funny hat, everybody sees you getting mad just like anybody else nun or no nun. Five days on this smelly bus how long you been on? Your whole life is a bus your convent is a bus you do it with the priests and janitors I've read all about you in the medical articles in the *papers,* lady. Pride goeth before, *I* know pride goeth before a fall, all I need is wings Lord I'd go with my pride and no one ever have a thing to say about it, specially nuns. You think I got problems? Honey lover baby angel, you got more problems figuring out what to do with that rose than I got in my whole fuckin life. She looked up and she was a woman sailing toward Pittsburgh on the bus, drunk, making a commotion like none she had ever made before.

The four motels of Jamie's experience had all been flat. They hadn't stood up to declare themselves for six storeys amid congested Pittsburgh, they had only reclined by their swimming pools taking the dust of the cars going by and Jamie did not care if the Hotel Magellan was a rotten hotel, peopled by escapees, with pocked, frayed carpeting and bedding that smelled of sorrow. It was a hotel, that was the important thing, and only seven blocks from the Golden Triangle, where the great buildings appeared ready to take off from Earth. Things were looking up, and she'd been gone from her husband only sixteen days. She thought it would be nice if they had a car.

"A car," Bill Houston said. He was standing before the bathroom door with a towel around his waist and a gigantic, completely naked black-haired woman all over his back whom he'd acquired in Singapore, in the Navy. He had navy tattoos and prison tattoos, and it was easy to tell which were which, because the navy ones were multi-colored and dazzling, while those from prison were faded to indistinct black smudges, like dirt. His mouth was open and his head thrust forward in a manner implying she should not talk any more about buying a car.

"Sure, why not a car?" Jamie said. She imagined pleasurable drives through the suburbs with Miranda Sue and Baby Ellen behaving nicely in the back seat, and the breezes of the new spring, not yet arrived, coming in through the windows of the car. "Save us all them taxis," she said. "All them buses." Miranda was dragging Baby Ellen all around the room exclaiming, "Lookit! Baby Ellen can finally walk." Jamie rescued the baby and laid her down on the bed.

"Well, what kind of a car?" Bill Houston said. "You mean like maybe a Chevy, or what?"

"Chevy'd be nice. That'd be just fine, Chevy or a Ford. Or whatever you want, Bill." It was his money.

He removed the towel from around his waist and started drying his hair. "Yeah? Well guess what," he said, and she asked him what, but he wouldn't tell her. He sat on the bed, where Baby Ellen lifted her head with difficulty and stared at him, her neck wavering unsteadily. Bill Houston stared at her blankly. The TV in a neighboring room blared momentarily at top volume, and then settled to a low murmur. A collection of saliva bubbles escaped from Baby Ellen's pursed lips. "She always looks like she's finally onto something real important," Bill Houston said. "But then all she ever does is spit all over herself." He stood up, and surveyed the room absently. "I got about two hunnerd left, that's what," he said.

"Oh," Jamie said. "That ain't a whole lot."

Bill Houston began to search the dresser for clothing. "Now, two hunnerd bucks, that'll get you maybe *part* of a semi-decent car. Or you can go to some smiley bastard on TV and go broke on a car that just don't run for shit." He pulled the bottom drawer out entirely and let it crash to the floor.

"Oh." She sat on the bed, sorry to have brought it up.

"Or," he said, "you could get you some food with it. That's in case you're the type of person who gets hungry every now and then. You ever get hungry?"

"I'm hungry now!" Miranda said.

"You shut up. I'm not talking to you now. You just had your lunch a half hour ago."

"Hush up now, hon," Jamie told Miranda. She caught hold of the child with the vague intention of embracing her, or braiding her hair. "Well. What all you going to do today?" she asked Bill Houston gaily.

"Don't go changing the subject on me," he said. "I had twenty-three hunnerd. I got two hunnerd left. What I want to find out —where the fuck did it all go?" He pulled in his stomach and cinched his belt.

Of course Pittsburgh was colder and wearier than Oakland, but it wasn't any filthier. What it seemed to lack that Oakland had was a sky. By day it looked like old newspapers had been pasted over the sun, and after dark the universe ended six feet above the tallest lamp. There were no dawns or sunsets in Pittsburgh; there were no heavens in which they might occur.

Tonight the stores on Irvine were still open, and they put enough light onto the sidewalks that Jamie could almost make out colors and tell the cares and joys on people's faces. She tried to enjoy it to the full: she knew that Irvine would turn into Second

Avenue—for Bill Houston, the door to intense merrymaking and oblivion.

Horrible gargoyles jutted from the walls around them. They moved along the sidewalk under the streetlamps, among the headlights, and Jamie shouted over the traffic noise, "Well I don't care if it *is* far. Let's us just go to Philadelphia. I never been there either. I never been any goddamn place."

"Now in my estimation," Bill Houston said, "there just ain't nothing in Philadelphia."

"Liberty Bell's something, ain't it? You going to tell me it's just nothing, just because it's in Philadelphia and you say there ain't nothing there?"

"The Liberty Bell ain't nothing to *do*. Ain't even anything to talk about. Talk about something else."

"It ain't so far to Philly," she said. "What about our *fore-fathers?*"

He began to draw ahead of her, a stranger to this woman a bit behind and to the left of him. "I would love to see the Washington Monument because it doesn't piss around. It's tall. One other thing is those four big statues of faces carved out of a mountain. But they ain't neither of them in Pittsburgh *or* Philly. Only thing in this state's the Liberty Bell, and that's just a bell—know what I mean? A bell."

"Well, it ain't far," Jamie pleaded. "I just wish we could go see it. It really ain't that far. It's patriotic."

"I was already patriotic for six years in the fuckin Navy," he said, grabbing a fistful of his purple cowboy shirt. "Anyway, *I* think it's too damn far. It's just crazy."

She saw she was ruining his evening, but couldn't keep from coaxing him as they moved down the block. He told her the Liberty Bell might be anywhere right now, maybe touring the country. He insisted they often took the Liberty Bell all around, parking it in schoolyards. Then he started telling her, "I just ain't

going to Philly. You can't get me to go there *no way!* Forget it!"
and she decided to talk instead about the Easter decorations
already displayed in the storefronts. "I don't have time for baskets
or rabbits," he said. "It costs too much money to go to Philly now.
We don't have enough time"—and she thought that he meant
they'd be finished when the money was finished. But they'd been
together only eleven days. She was sorry to have ruined his evening.

They walked in silence for a time and then she asked casually,
"Hey—how much you got left these days, anyway?"—but breath-
lessly, too, winded from their walking.

"I think there's a good country band up here a ways," he said.
"Ga-damn, I'd like to see Waylon Jennings. I saw Johnny Cash
when I was in the joint, but I never have seen Waylon."

"Well, maybe we hadn't ought to go there tonight," she said.
"Maybe we ought to save that band for another night, huh? What
do you think about it?"

"What. Think about what."

"Think we ought to save Waylon for another night, Bill?"

"I never said Waylon was playing at this place. You think
Waylon Jennings is going to play at one of these piss factories?
Use your brain."

"But what I mean to say is, you don't have a whole lot left, do
you? Didn't you pay the hotel tonight? I thought you paid—"

"Yeah, I did. You got to pay them or you can't stay there. They
insist on it."

"Oh. For a day's worth?"

"The most important thing you can do right now," he said, "is
be quiet."

"Oh. Uh-oh." She looked away from his bobbing shoulder. She
looked at the street. I am ruining this evening.

"I guess I got like a hunnerd and ten left. Something like that,"
Bill Houston said.

"Oh," she said, hurrying to catch up to him and look into his face. "Well, maybe we just better go home," she said. "If that's what you feel like, it's okay with me, because we don't have to go out ever single night."

"No. Let's just step inside of here a minute. And then we'll take the bus to this one other place I was telling you about." And abruptly he was in fine spirits. "Oh, come on! What you think —you can't have you a good time on a hunnerd and ten bones? Well you just step in through here with me, little Miss, and we'll see about it."

They stopped at several other bars where Bill Houston drank large and Jamie watched as if scrutinizing a mystery, rarely joining him. She felt she was falling apart with weariness, but Bill Houston seemed oblivious to the whole idea of the Hotel Magellan. "Right here. This is what we been after all along," he said, gesturing at the entrance of the Tally Ho Budweiser King of Beers. In the window beneath this sign, neon blinked BUD—BUD —BUD. "We're here to stay."

"Now, hey—this ain't the one you were telling about." She held back. "This one doesn't even have a band playing or nothing. All they got is Budweiser Beer, looks like. Probably don't even have a bar."

"This is a fine place," he said. "We'll go in this fine place right here."

"You don't even know this place," she told him.

"This is a fine place," he said.

"I don't think you ever been here before."

"Listen here," he said. "I grew up here practically. This is practically my home. It was a fine home." With a hand he influenced her through the door.

Immediately Jamie disliked its insides. There were unescorted women at the bar itself, drinking glumly with their chins sticking out. There were innumerable sounds—low voices, chairs moved, a voice rising with passion and then subsiding—but in her frayed weariness Jamie felt that these were a continual breaking of a general stunned silence, and she was tempted to whisper as in a hospital. "We ought to go back and see what's happening on the television," she said not loudly, and Bill Houston cast her a look. "I'm awful tarred right now," she insisted. They sat down at a table toward the front. In the back a man pounded on his table, spilling a drink, and the woman who was with him suddenly got up and left, her earrings jiggling as she marched away stiffly. All around them men drank alone, staring out of their faces. They'd been here twenty seconds, and already nothing was happening. Nobody came to their table to take their order. A man came over and tried to take Jamie away from Bill Houston. He pointed to the woman he was with, over at the bar, and offered to trade.

"I knew this would happen," Jamie said.

"This is the third time I've picked her up—over at the Far East Lounge," the man explained, pointing again to the woman at the bar. The woman was scratching her throat with a pinky while looking at herself in the mirror. Bill Houston listened politely.

"Oh, she's all right," the man said quickly. "Nothing wrong with her. Just I've hung out with her before is all, about six times, and she tells the same old jokes. But they'd be new to you, right? What do you say?" He turned to Jamie. "What do you say? You don't mind."

"I most certainly—Bill! Will you tell him what's what?" She pulled Kleenex from her purse and started wiping at her make-up. She shifted in her chair and yanked at the hem of her skirt.

The man smiled. "She seems stuck on you," he told Bill Houston. "But she won't mind. You won't mind, will you? She won't mind. What do you say, old buddy?"

"Well now, I don't exactly know," Bill Houston said. "All depends. How much you say you're paying that lady?"

"Oh, there's no—it's very unofficial," the man said. "We haven't really gotten around to that yet. She just wants, you know, a present. It all depends."

"Hey. I don't know if this is a joke, or what," Jamie said excitedly. "You stop it. Listen, I can't use this. What are you doing?"

The man seemed to sense complications. His smile turned wary.

"You think this one's worth fifty?" Bill Houston asked him.

"Bill!" Jamie caught hold of his arm and clawed it frantically, remaining stiff and erect in her chair.

The man began looking Jamie over. Bill Houston smiled off toward the shadows.

"Oh, yeah, definitely—fifty dollars," the man said.

She didn't want to draw stares by rising from her place. She covered her face with her hands. *"Bill,"* she said, into her hands.

"Well now, you were the one crying about money just a while ago." Then he laughed with embarrassment.

Jamie found herself, behind her hands, considering the amount of fifty dollars. "Stop. Stop. Please," she said into her hands.

The man stood uncomfortably beside their table, and put his own hands in his pockets.

"Okay," Bill Houston said. "Guess that's that. Just a misunderstanding. Nobody's fault. Right?" he said to the man.

"Oh, hell—a misunderstanding?" the man said. He looked at Bill Houston. "Oh, listen, say, I guess I—boy, I'm sure sorry." He turned very red even in the dim light, and left their table. He took the woman at the bar by the arm and went out with her, lifting a hand weakly to Jamie while staring angrily at Bill Houston. The woman went where she was urged, trying repeatedly, and failing, to get her purse-strap hooked over her shoulder.

Jamie and Bill Houston said nothing. The bartender came over to their table with two Seven-and-Sevens, compliments of the mistaken gentleman. Jamie wanted to leave right away. Bill Houston downed both drinks and they went out.

They said nothing for a while on the street. Jamie halted at a bus stop on the side of the street pointing home. Bill Houston walked on in apparent ignorance of her stopping, then turned and went back to stand with her, as if puzzled why she was no longer in a partying mood. After a while Bill Houston breathed deeply of the night and then exhaled, saying, "Aaaaaaah!" And then he stretched and yawned and said, "Hey there!" and "Well now!" and other such things.

The bus had passed through Homewood, then Brushton; they'd missed their stop a long, long time ago. Jamie rested her head against the back of the seat and read all the advertisements above the windows. Bill Houston was up at the front of the bus, standing there with his arm wrapped around the silver pole and leaning over as if looking for something he'd dropped in the driver's lap. "Listen. Got a proposition for you," he was telling the driver.

"No," the driver said. "Nope, no propositions. I just can't listen to any propositions." He was a compact young man with a boot-camp style crew-cut under an official bus driver's hat supported solely by his ears. It was plain he didn't want to talk to Bill Houston.

"You got nothing better to do than listen to me," Bill Houston said. "Ain't nothing else happening. We're the only ones on your bus."

The driver glanced around and touched the buttons of his shirt with the fingers of one hand. "Look. There's certain rules on this bus," he said.

"Course there's rules! Has to be rules to make everything work out right, right?"

The driver rubbed his chin, unwilling to agree too hastily.

"Certainly!" Bill Houston said. "Hey, I learned all about rules in the Navy. When it comes to rules, you just listen to me."

"I'm not listening," the driver said. "You can't get me to listen."

Jamie imagined a great blade protruding for miles from her window, levelling the whole suburbs six feet above the ground. She sat there waiting for Bill Houston to get arrested.

Bill Houston rode the floor of the bus like the pitching and heaving deck of a great ship. "There has to be rules to make things run right," He was explaining, *"but.* If you got an idea about breaking the rules to make things run *better,* why goddamn it then a course there ain't a reason in the world not to break the rules."

"I don't know. Look—what are we talking about?" the driver said.

"Now, here it is: I'm going to pay you a little extra to take this bus where we want to get to, that's all. I'll pay you all the extra you want."

"Never happen." The driver shook his head. His hat seemed to stay in one place while his head moved from side to side beneath it. He stopped at a light and put his elbow on the steering and his chin in his hand.

"What! Wait up one second," Bill Houston said. "I ain't even said where we're going yet. This is a winner. Going to make you a lot of extra cash. You want to listen?"

"No sir. Don't want to listen." The driver removed his hat and put both hands over his ears.

Fishing several dollars from his wallet, Bill Houston held them before the driver's face. The driver shook his head.

"Okay, I'll name you a figure," Bill Houston said. The figure was thrown from his heart, from the depths of his body: "Fifty bones."

The driver took his hands from his ears and drew a small printed sheet from the shelf below his steering wheel. "I got my specific route right here," he said. He snapped the paper several times with his finger. "This is it. If I don't see it on here, then it just isn't it. That's all."

Bill Houston took all the money from his wallet and held it out to the driver like a bouquet. "Tell you where to point this thing," he said. "We want to see the Liberty Bell. Over in Philly."

The driver's eyes grew wide. "Sure. One in the morning."

"Right here"—Bill Houston thumbed the money—"right here is, here is, here is—ninety-six dollars! Ninety-six big old big ones, boy. Now how much you make tonight all night, driving down your specific route there? Don't seem exactly like the big time, does it?"

The driver looked over his printed sheet carefully, as if hoping to find that Philadelphia had become part of his route.

Bill Houston fanned his sheaf of money. "Ninety-six dollars."

"*I* know how much it is. It's just that I'd be out of a job. I'd lose this job for sure."

"You won't need no job, with ninety-six dollars."

"Philadelphia!" the young driver said.

"You got it! You're getting it! The Liberty Bell! Which my poor wife sitting right over there has always wanted to see, poor woman, and she never has seen it yet, poor little old gal. And she's dying. Got a disease, if you want to know the truth. Ninety-six dollars!"

"Now, hold up a minute," Jamie said from her seat, but Bill Houston waved her off. She said nothing else, waiting to see how far this whole show was headed.

"I just can't *go* anywhere I want to with a crazy man to Philly," the driver said. "Philadelphia!" He put his hat back on his head. He checked his hand brake. He looked at his watch. "Standing in front of the white line," he said in a neutral tone, pointing down at the line. "Delaying the bus driver. Attempted bribery."

"What? What is this?" Bill Houston slammed his palm against the metal pole and made it ring. "Right in the middle of negotiations you're handing me the goddamn rules. Don't you know when the world is trying to do you a kindness?"

"Talking to the driver. Trying to get the driver to go off his specific route," the driver said.

"Ninety-six dollars," Bill Houston said. The driver put his bus in gear.

"Now you turn this bus off," Bill Houston said, "and let's talk."

"Just please wait one minute," Jamie put in. "Hold up there," she said good-naturedly. Nobody was listening. Bill Houston had taken a pint bottle of Gordon's Gin from his pants pocket and was waving it around in the area of his mouth.

The driver was maneuvering his bus around a circle with a lawn and a big ugly statue in its midst. "Consuming alcoholic beverages on the bus! Standing in front of the white line talking to the driver with ninety-six dollars attempted bribery!"

"Goddamn *I'll* show you ninety-six dollars bribing." Bill Houston moved his face and his fistful of money in front of the driver's face. The driver continued driving his bus, leaning to one side to see past Bill Houston's head and hand. "I don't *want* this money, see?" Bill Houston said. "I just don't give a shit about this money. Do you give a shit about this money?"

"*I* do!" Jamie said. "Bill! Sit down!"

"You better leave me alone—right now," the driver told him. "You're disturbing the other passengers on my bus."

"Okay," Bill Houston said. "*You* don't give a shit about this money. *I* don't give a shit about this money. Okay. All right, that's just perfectly okay with me." He placed the bills in a pile on the floor beside the driver's seat. Jamie and the driver looked on as he adjusted the flame on his Bic butane and then set the money afire.

Jamie wailed terribly.

The driver wanted to watch the street and Bill Houston with amazed eyes both at once, turning his head rapidly from front to side. "Burning money! On the bus! My Christ! A fucking lunatic! Get away from that white line!"

Jamie had leaped forward to save the money. She stamped on it repeatedly, shouting along with the driver. Bill Houston was ready, the flame on his butane set high as possible, and he blocked her feet with his arm as he knelt by the pile of dollars, ravaging it with flame. Jamie managed to snatch the top few bills from the pile and held them tightly in her fist, but the rest was charred past rescue.

The driver stopped his bus and opened the door, and the three of them regarded the black smoldering heap until it was ash and the smoke had all blown out the door, and the bus ride was definitely over. "Guess nobody's going to Philly now," the driver said.

Jamie ran out of the bus. Bill Houston watched her. "Now look what happened," he told the driver, flabbergasted, leaving.

They stood on the sidewalk surrounded by a windswept and desolate shopping mall in Lincoln Park. It looked like a nice place to drive around in, in the daytime, if you had a car. Jamie had saved thirteen dollars. She was seized with a desire to run back to the dingy bar and find the man who had valued her at fifty. Bill Houston was experimenting with his Bic butane lighter, holding it upside down and trying to keep it lighted. "The gas wants to go up," he explained to her, "but then it has to go down before it can go up. It don't know what to do." When it exploded in his hand, he stared at his torn fingers through eyes spattered with blood, looking like he didn't know what to do. He turned to her, astonished, wanting some kind of endorsement, some kind of confirmation. "Did you see that?"

"Your fingers are all tore up," she said.

"That's what I mean. That's exactly what I'm saying."

"Did you burn your hand, too?" Jamie said.

He said, "Did I burn it? Yeah I burnt it."

"Does it hurt?" she said.

"Does it hurt?" he said. "You can't imagine."

He blew on his fingers and then shook them as if trying to get a bug off his hand. Then he held his hand in his other hand and pretended he wasn't crying. Jamie took wadded pieces of Kleenex from her purse and tried to straighten them out and administer them to the wounded fingers, but the wind blew them away and they went scudding along the sidewalk. "This kind of shit just keeps happening until you're dead," Bill Houston told her. They took a cab to the nearest Emergency Room. Bill Houston took up the middle of the seat, chuckling now and then in disbelief, staring at the injured hand in his lap as if to find any kind of hand there at all was unexpected and portentous. Jamie leaned up against the left-hand window, snuffling and crying and looking out at the shut avenues hard, as if only a little while ago she had owned them.

Every time she did the laundry she threw away some of the clothes. One of everything: less to wash, less to carry, less to know about. She threw four pairs of socks into the trash. One of her bras didn't look right: she threw it away. "Listen, you want this suitcase?" she told a man standing there. He looked like a bum who was on vacation from destitution. But he didn't want her suitcase.

She was looking at her children and hating them when a black woman opened up one of the big driers and took out her child, a little boy about three. "More, Mama?" he said. "More? More?"

The woman sat him on the floor and he staggered about. Jamie couldn't believe it. The woman tried to fold her clothes, but her little boy grabbed hold of the hem of her skirt as if he would climb right up her. "More, Mama? Mama? Mama? More." Annoyed, the woman picked him up with one arm and put him back into the drier. She slugged in a dime and shut the door and went back to folding clothes.

Miranda approached her mother, wide-eyed, looking ready to speak, pointing to the driers. "Don't even think about it," Jamie told her. "I'll let you know when it gets that bad."

Jamie lay flat on her back on the green table. If she stared at the white acoustic tiles of the ceiling and kind of let her eyes go loose, the pattern would shift and the tiles would seem to draw down on her until she was inside of them. There was nothing else to do right about now.

She was the only woman in this row of tables. In the entire room, which was the size of a ballroom, there were four women and nearly fifty men, each stretched out on a green table with a green sheet, getting a good look at the ceiling. Out in the large anteroom, a couple of hundred others looked at the television or studied the floor, waiting to be attached to plastic bags and drained of five dollars' worth of blood plasma.

Jamie didn't like any of it. If she let her eyes go too loose, checking out the tiles above, she started crying.

A man in a white coat was going down her row, jabbing everybody with a needle and getting their blood to shoot through a tube into a quart-sized plastic bag that sat on a scales beside each table. He came to Jamie, smiling like a leopard. She shut her eyes and thought about the beach. "First time?" the man said, and Jamie said nothing. "Give your fist a squeeze about once per second," the man said.

"Ow! You nailing my arm to the bed, or what?"

"Relax," the man said, doing things with tubes and tape. Jamie thought of the beach, the water filled with surfers in wetsuits in the wintertime, all of them waiting for a great wave to lift and carry them toward the deserted Santa Cruz amusement park. In a minute she let one eye sneak open and watched the blood fill her plastic bag as once per second she relaxed her fist and then closed it tightly. The blood was bright red at first, but it grew darker, nearly black, as the bag fattened. The scales tipped when the bag held a pint. She heard others around her telling the nurses, "I'm full," "I'm full," and when another nurse, a woman, came near, Jamie said, "I'm full."

The nurse smelled of alcohol and talcum as she bent over Jamie's bag of blood. She put the bag on a smaller scales that she carried with her and said, "Not quite full. Pump a little more." Jamie didn't see how one set of scales knew more than another. She opened and closed her fist several times. "All . . . right," the nurse said, and Jamie quit. The nurse removed Jamie's tourniquet and adjusted stoppers and tubes. "You're going to feel the saline solution coming into your arm now," the nurse said. "That's just to keep the vein open." She clamped and cut the tube that led into the blood, and carried the bag away to another room, where the plasma would be removed somehow.

Jamie thought her blood looked like good earth, rich and full and wet. "Used to take goldfish home from the carnival in plastic bags like that," she told the departing nurse, who didn't hear. She began shivering all over as the cool saline mixed into her system.

The man on her left said, "Fuck goldfish. Fuck 'em." He was a bearded old guy and he was shaking like a machine.

The man on her right said, "Did you know this? Frogs fuck goldfish. That's true. No fooling, now."

"Hey," Jamie said. "I can't use that talk. Be a gentleman, how about."

"How about if I whip it out and piss on you?" the man said. "How's that for a gentleman?"

Jamie didn't say anything. She decided to stab him with her nail file later on, on the way out.

The bearded old man on her left said, "Don't pay no attention to these guys." He turned toward her onto his side, careful not to disturb the needle in his vein. "Most of them," he said, "are just wooden people." His face seemed to be rotting away on him. His eyes were shiny as a blind man's.

Jamie said nothing, but the man wanted to talk. "Most of the people you see are just wooden men," he told her, his voice quaking as if he'd cry in a minute. "They're dead people, walking around like the living."

"Yeah," Jamie said. "I noticed that myself."

"You have?" The man was excited. "Then you're one of the living." He licked his mouth convulsively. "There's not too many of us. We haven't got much time. Are you filled in on the whole story?"

"What whole story? Hey. You're bothering me."

"I'm not bothering you. I'm saving your life. Your life is the truth. Listen: The world was made in 1914. Before 1914 there was nothing. Eleven people are in charge of the world. They make up the news and the history books, they control everything you think you know. They wrote the Bible and all the other books. Most people are wooden people, controlled by remote control. There's only a few of us who are real, and we're getting *fooled.*"

"I can't use this," Jamie said. "I mean, I'm just here trying to get some lunch money."

"The world is flat. It's two hundred and fifty-six square miles in area, sixteen by sixteen. When you go someplace on a plane, what they do is, they just use their powers inside your mind to make you *think* like the time is passing. To make you *think* you're getting somewhere."

The nurse came back wheeling a cart piled high with plastic sacks of blood. She read the label on Jamie's and said, "Name please?"

"They do things inside your *mind,*" the man whispered to Jamie.

"My name is Jamie Mays," she told the nurse.

The nurse showed her the name on the label—*Jamie Mays*—

and Jamie nodded, and the old man whispered, "They're putting new memories into us right now."

The nurse hung the blood up next to the saline solution and adjusted the tubes and stoppers, and one tube turned bright crimson as it fed Jamie's own blood, minus plasma, back into her. "New memories is what's inside that bag," the man announced calmly.

"Great," Jamie said. "I was sick of the old ones."

"In Malaya, I killed a little Chink. Supposedly Malaya. I broke his head apart," the man said.

"Jesus Christ," Jamie told the ceiling.

"There were machines inside his head," the man said quietly.

"Everybody in this town—they're all the same," Jamie told the ceiling.

"That's what I mean!"

"No—I mean—oh, forget it."

"There was machine stuff inside his head. He wasn't a real person."

"Why don't you quit? I can't use that baloney right now."

"Everywhere you go, it's the same people. Don't you see what's happening to your life, woman?"

"Not exactly," Jamie said.

"You're going to see, all right. Something is happening to your life, and you're going to see what it is."

"I was afraid of that," Jamie said.

"If you think you're afraid now," the man said.

2

Bill Houston's elbows on the bar were numb. He couldn't feel his mouth in his face. Respectfully he held his injured hand aloft, as if ready for some arm-wrestling. It was bandaged and sewn up like a teddy bear's, but its throbbing was distant and nothing like pain. From the high place that was his head he looked down at the drink in front of him and saw that its ice was melted, a sign he was slowing down, because when he was drinking seriously he wasted no time and there was always plenty of ice banging around inside the glass when he was finished. "Hey—what is this place, anyways?" he asked the bartender. "What's the name of this place?"

The bartender was very rapidly washing beer glasses two at a time, sticking them down into the suds and then into the rinse water, and then setting them in neat rows on a towel laid out by the sink. The bartender said, "Say what?"

"I says what is the name of this place?"

The bartender puffed a sigh upward, as if trying to blow his hair away from his eyes. But he was bald. "This bar has the electrifying name of Joe's Bar," he said.

"No—but what *town* is it, I mean to say. What *town.*"

"Don't ask," the bartender said. "You don't want to know."

"Fair enough. Okay," Bill Houston said.

He watched the bartender wash glasses. He was always fascinated by small, deft movements of the hands and arms. His own arms were wrecked. His elbows made popping noises when he flexed them, and his fingers were blunt and misshapen. High living had worked some kind of bad influence on his nerves and caused his hands to quake and rattle when spooning sugar into coffee or raising a glass to his mouth. But he could lift the rear wheels of a V-8 Ford entirely off the ground. "I can't feel my face," he told the bartender. It took him a long time to say words.

"That's the whole idea, isn't it?"

"Can't exactly feel the rest of my body, neither."

"So? You complaining?"

Bill Houston knew that way of talking. "I'll make you a bet," he said. "Bet I can ask just one more question, and then I'll know what town you got here."

The bartender seemed to be ignoring him.

"Hey—does a bus stop out front there every now and then?"

"Well," the bartender said, "it ain't gonna come in *here* for you."

Bill Houston guffawed, thumped the bar, pointed a triumphant finger at the bartender like the barrel of a gun: "Chicago!"

. . .

He was in the back of a spacious, empty establishment trying to woo a large woman named Gail Ann, for whom he was experiencing a tender fascination. They danced. Bill Houston was clumsy, and when they danced nearer the bowling game, he put in a quarter and began flinging the metal puck at the plastic pins hanging down from above the board. David Allan Coe sang on the jukebox as they traded glances across the width of the bowling game, alternately bold and shy glances. They sat at a small round table in the back, talking low, head-to-head. It was an orange table that made him think of things from outer space.

Now Hank Williams, Jr., began singing out of the jukebox like a swan, and Bill Houston's heart grew large and embraced the universe. He wondered if the jukeboxes of all cafes and barrooms were owned by the Mafia, like they told you, and he wondered at all the juke-joints he'd walked into, marvelled at the number of them, saw every narrow dance floor stretched out end to end in a panorama not of what he'd traversed, but of what lay before him, as if it were his past he must start living now and not his future; and he asked Gail Ann, "Gail Ann, what time is it?" It was a question weighted with desperation, because he was seized suddenly with the idea there was not very much time. He grasped his drink more firmly. It was cold to the touch.

Gail Ann told him she didn't have the slightest idea what time it was. She would get herself another beer maybe and find that out. She went in the direction of the bar, but walked right on past it to the coatrack, grabbed her coat, and strolled out the door into Chicago. The door had one of those vacuum devices on it that prevent slamming, and Bill Houston watched it shut quietly and slowly. He caught a glimpse of Gail Ann's coat unfurling behind her as she threw it around her shoulders and the door closed. There was a wall-poster on this side of the door, an autographed picture of Frank Sinatra over the legend, "Old Blue-Eyes Is Back." Bill Houston nodded goodbye to Frank Sinatra.

· · ·

The wind was coming down from the North Pole, travelling across the flat of Canada for a thousand miles to slap him in the face as if he were a child. Wilson Street was covered with innumerable bits of trash that picked up and set down in flocks like paper birds feeding alongside the buildings. Bill Houston went, "Oooooooh!"—meaning to launch into a song, like a drunken sailor, but he faded off, forgetting what to sing. He wasn't a sailor any more anyway. He was just a fool on the move, no less bitter than the wind. He was an ex-sailor, and an ex-offender—though he couldn't, for the life of him, say who it was he had offended —and he was an ex-husband—three ex-husbands, actually—and he'd been parted from his money and from Jamie in Pittsburgh, spending like the sailor he no longer was, slapping Jamie's little darling Miranda—who would almost certainly grow up to become a cheap sleaze—and spending fifty percent of their time together in an alcoholic blackout. Where had Chicago come from? It frightened him in his mind to wake up in unexpected towns with great holes in his recollection, particularly to understand that he'd been doing things, maybe *committing* things: his body mobilizing itself, perhaps changing his life all around, making raw deals he would someday have to pay the ticket for.

He rested with his back flat against a building, and had the sensation of lying down when he was standing up. The streets swung back and forth like a bell. No doubt about it, it was a dizzy life. Something was missing here. When he was dry, he believed it was alcohol he needed, but when he had a few drinks in him, he knew it was something else, possibly a woman; and when he had it all—cash, booze, and a wife—he couldn't be distracted from the great emptiness that was always falling through him and never hit the ground. He should have gotten a damn *job* in Pittsburgh! He began to cry, each sob coming up slowly like something with a hook on it. Tears on his cheeks burned in the cold wind. Rolling his head from side to side against the bricks he hollered, "I wanna meet my *responsibilities!*" But in the commotion of city traffic it sounded like the tiniest thing he'd ever said, and he got going down the street.

Bill Houston was trying to draw near behind two women in overcoats carrying purses. His feet were a couple of burdens he yanked along because there was no discarding them. He wasn't ready for this move, actually, but the energy would come to him when he was near enough: reach and get a fist around each purse-strap, hold tight and bust between the two of them like a couple of swinging doors, leaving them spinning on the sidewalk while he disappeared with their purses from their lives. He trawled along behind while the rush of fear dried his mouth and straightened his head. His legs and feet were coming to life.

He stood up straight, walking like a man again, taking in all the sights along Wilson. The street was all yellow in the artificial light. People were walking up and down it like a lot of fools. It was around nine-thirty, there was a chill in the air, the wind was gentle now, and he was moving inside it like the light of love, ringing without sound, giving himself up to every vibration, totally alive inside of a crime. The women turned down Clark and the song of the thief grew slow and mellow, beating like a bass viol now because the time and place were suddenly all wrong for a purse-snatch, and the real crime was not yet revealed.

He slowed with the rhythm of it all. The two women drifted farther ahead of him. He was relaxed, letting the whole thing happen, floating into a little hardware place crammed with everything necessary for the good life, including shelves of lumber. One man behind the counter—a young gentleman wearing an orange apron—dealing with one male purchaser and the purchaser's two children, a boy and a girl who yanked on his arms and blew large pink bubbles out of their mouths. Bill Houston drifted along each of five aisles in turn. Gleaming pastel commode seats hung from the back wall. Plumbing accessories, assorted tools, screws, and nails, metal shelves, everything burning with an inner flame. From the back of one aisle he examined the clerk, messing him over with his eyes. Young. Disgusted. Pocket full of pens in his orange apron, sideburns, heavy-framed spectacles bespeaking sincerity. Hundreds of times, almost daily, he had lived this robbery in his mind, making all the right moves, playing the hero, beating the thief senseless and shrugging it all off as the police slammed the doors of the van. Bill Houston knew him like he knew himself. In this state of things Bill Houston claimed all the power.

The people left. Nobody else in the place. Everything was as solid as a diamond.

"Whatta you need tonight?" the kid called down the aisle.

"How much is this here?" Bill Houston held up a plumber's helper.

The kid was disgusted. "I got ten thousand a dese items in here," he said. "You think I got every price memorized?" He came around the counter and walked down the aisle.

Bill Houston moved to meet him halfway, his finger jamming up his coat pocket. The kid looked surprised a second, and Bill Houston grabbed him by the throat with his free hand, sticking the pocket-finger into the kid's crotch, slamming him up against the shelves. "You motherfucker!" Bill told him. "You piss-ant kike! You're a dead motherfucker! You've lived the slimiest fucking life you could live and now it's *over!*" He could feel each hair and pore of himself as he spoke. Every tiny thing in the place cried out with the fire of God.

The clerk had no words on this occasion. He was going limp, so Bill Houston drew out his bandaged and swollen gun-hand and slapped him a couple of times. He turned the clerk around and kicked his butt down the aisle to the cash register. *"Get* the fuck around there you dead mother*fucker!* I want every dollar you can get your hands on and I want it now! Not *later.* You understand, dead man?"

The kid whipped open the cash register and started laying out the contents rapidly. He was all white, and his lips were turning purple. "Go! Go! Go! I'm clocking your ass!" Bill Houston watched him move. Time to shift gears. "You're doing fine," Houston told him softly. "You're gonna live through this. You're doing just like I tell you, you're saving your life, we're gonna get you through this alive. One pile for the bills, that's right, now a bag for the change. Double-bag it. Good strong bag. Good boy, good boy, good boy."

The clerk was doing all right, but he dropped the bags trying to get one inside the other, and had to stoop down to pick one up. Bill grabbed him by the hair and yanked him to his feet. *"Move!* Do like I *tell* you! You're dying!" The kid got a grip and did correctly with the two bags. He poured the change into them and as if in a trance picked up his stapler, folded the bags, and fastened them shut with two staples: snap, snap. Bill Houston loved it. He put the bills in his pocket, grabbed the kid's apron front, and threw him onto the floor. "I want you to pray," he said softly. "Pray for your life. Pray for a long time. Pray I don't come back." On the floor, beside the counter, the kid looked a little confused. "Pray." The kid took his glasses off, and looked at them. "Put your hands together and pray," Bill told him. The kid put his hands together, holding his glasses between them. "Pray loud, so I can hear you."

"Our Father, Who art in Heaven," the kid whispered.

"Louder," Bill Houston said, stepping out the door.

He could hear the clerk saying, "Our Father, Who art in Heaven, oh, Jesus Christ, oh, Jesus Christ," as he headed rapidly up Clark.

Ten PM, and the town of Chicago was shining. He moved up Wilson and into the El station, paid his fare and was up on the platform at the best possible moment, ducking into a train one second before the doors shut.

The lives of strangers lashed out at him through their windows as the train sailed down to the Loop. He witnessed their checkered tablecloths and the backs of their heads and the images moving on their television screens like things trapped under ice. The train was warm, the light was right.

He realized that he was the greatest thief of all time.

The knowledge seemed to rise unendurably and then break inside of him, and he sat by the train's window inhabiting a calm open space in the night. He sat still while his heart slowed down, moving where the train moved, listening to it talk to the tracks, feeling all right, letting the love pour through him over the world.

He opened his eyes.

He was lying on his back, his bandaged left hand resting carefully on his chest, the right one wrapped around the neck of a bottle of gin. He didn't need a map or a clock to tell him he was in the wrong place at the wrong time again. It was three AM, and he was now a resident of the senselessly named Dunes Hotel on Diversy, floor number three. When he sat up and put his feet on the cold floor, the darkness seemed to rush up suddenly against his face and stop there, palpitating rapidly like the wings of a moth. He went over by the window and sat in the wooden chair and took a look out into the street, putting the bottle's mouth to his lips and letting the gin touch his tongue, overcome by an acute sensitivity to everything. The few colors visible on the street seemed to burn. He could feel even the ridges of his fingerprints on the lukewarm bottle. The street out there was a mess of things —trash and rust and grease—all holding still for a minute. In his mind he was wordless, knowing what the street was and who he was, the man with the fingerprints looking out at the street, one bare foot resting on a shoe and the other flat on the chilly linoleum, a drunk and deluded man without a chance. It was all right to be who he was, but others would probably think it was terrible. A couple of times in the past he'd reached this absolute zero of the truth, and without fear or bitterness he realized now that somewhere inside it there was a move he could make to change his life, to become another person, but he'd never be able to guess what it was. He found a cigaret and struck a match—for a moment there was nothing before him but the flame. When he shook it out and the world came back, it was the same place again where all his decisions had been made a long time ago.

Jamie could feel the muscles in her leg jerk, she wanted so badly to kick Miranda's rear end and send her scooting under the wheels of, for instance, a truck. Clark Street at nine PM was a movie: five billion weirdos walking this way and that not looking at each other, and every third one had something for sale. Moneylickers; and black pimps dressed entirely in black, and a forest of red high heels. There were lots of lights—everyone had half a dozen shadows scurrying in different directions underneath them.

Paced to Jamie's exhaustion, the scene moved in slow motion. A black youth in a knit cap, long coat and white tennis shoes bopped by, smiling at her and then looking away and singing, "Time for us to go get high, hmmmmmmmmm?"—and moving on when Jamie said nothing. Baby Ellen was awake in her mother's arms, protesting even a moment's consignment to her infant seat, and the little black balls in the midst of her eyes tracked the youth's passage serenely and mechanically. For a second Jamie was struck with the peculiar notion that this scene of downtown Chicago was the projection of her daughter's infant mind.

Jamie had her reasons for being here. She just couldn't think what they were, at the moment. She had waved Bill Houston goodbye as he'd boarded his bus back to Chicago in a state of hopeless inebriation, suddenly convinced in his mind that something or other awaited him among these sorry strangers. Jamie, for her part, had still had possession of two tickets to Hershey, and she'd waited around a few days—first until a loan from her sister-in-law had arrived, and then longer, until it was nearly spent—and then she'd seen the uselessness of everything and had realized that she had a few words to say to Bill Houston. His departure had looked like the end of their involvement. But it was not the end. You got so you could feel these things.

Now she stood on Clark Street out of ideas. Miranda straddled the suitcase, riding it like a horse. There weren't any hotel-type monstrosities in sight. Some of these theaters looked all right, and some of them looked like X-rated. The two or three restaurants she could see were closed. A bitter wind seemed to blow the light around among the buildings. None of these people they were among now looked at all legitimate.

"Ma-ma," Miranda said, "Ma-ma, Ma-ma, Ma-ma"—just chanting, tired and confused. A man in a cheap and ridiculous red suit standing two yards away seemed to be taking an unhealthy interest in her as she bounced on the suitcase. "Come here, hon," Jamie said, yanking her off it by the arm. The man kept looking at them. "You are sick," she told him. The El train screeched around a curve in the tracks a half block away. Everything suddenly seemed submerged in deafness. "Shit," Jamie said. "My eyeballs feel like boiling rocks."

"What?" Miranda peered up at the shadow of her mother's face. "Lemme see, Mama."

The man in the red suit had approached. "Good evening." Hands jammed in his pockets; collar turned up.

"I hate this part," Jamie said. "I hate the part where the hilljack in the red suit says good evening."

"I'm not a hilljack," the man said. "I know everybody from here to about six blocks north of Wilson."

"I lack the strength to talk to you," Jamie said.

"Well, I just thought I could probably help you." He gestured, palm up, toward Miranda, and the suitcase, and then the baby in Jamie's arms, as if introducing her to her difficulty. "I drank two cups of coffee in the lounge there"—with the same hand, he now included the bus station behind them among her troubles—"and you were just kind of hanging around inside the door the whole time. Now you're *out*side the door. I mean, are you waiting for somebody? What's your story?" He had a thinly nervous quality of innocence—he seemed, all of a sudden, not too dangerous.

"I haven't got a story," Jamie said. "I'm on empty."

"I really don't care what you think of my suit," the man said. "I don't have to explain anything to anybody about my suit. I'm on Voke Rehab, is the thing. I have a disease. I don't need to work or buy or sell. Do you know what?" he said to Miranda. "All I ever do is go in one joint after another, and talk to the people about anything—whatever they want to talk about. That's how I know everybody from here to Wilson and beyond. So I wanted to help your mother, but she just thinks I'm a hilljack in a red suit or something. Is this one a boy or a girl?" he asked Jamie, peering closely into the shadowed face of Baby Ellen, wrapped in a blanket and nestled in her mother's arms. "Got black eyes."

"Girl," Jamie said.

"If you're waiting for somebody," the man said, "they're sure taking their time, whoever they are. Are you waiting for somebody?"

"I'm looking for somebody. Not waiting. Looking."

"Who are you looking for? Jeez, it's cold. Let's get out of this winter." He pushed backward through the glass doors of the station, dragging the suitcase with both hands, drawing Jamie and Miranda after him as if by the influence of a galactic wind. "Who are you looking for?" In the brighter illumination, his suit was revealed to be absolutely, absolutely red. "Who you seeking? Your boyfriend."

"Bill Houston!" Miranda said.

"Bill Houston? I know him."

"Like I know the Pope," Jamie said. "You know my mother too?"

"Kind of a big guy, right? Maybe not exactly big, I mean, not *huge.* Got a tattoo on this arm? Or maybe this arm, I don't remember."

Regarding him now with a riveted awareness, Jamie saw that he wore his blond hair all the same length, brandished in all possible directions from his scalp like an electric flame. His suit was the little Elvis Costello kind. He was just trying to be on-the-minute. He was not an unfamiliar specimen.

"Pretty weird that I know him, huh? I told you, I know everyone." He wandered, with an aura of the victor, over to the row of nickel vending machines against the wall of tiny yellowed tiles. Casually he perused the offerings there: oversized balls of chewing gum; toy finger jewelry and idiot spiders in their individual clear plastic capsules.

"Get me a gum, okay?" Miranda said, trailing after him. "Can I have a piece of gum? It's only one nickel."

"Hey," Jamie said, walking over after some hesitation. "You're just power-tripping me here, and I don't like it."

"What do you mean? I said I could help you and you said I couldn't. But I really can. That must tell you something. Right?"

Holding the baby in her left arm, Jamie put the fingers of her right hand to her eyes and pushed firmly, obliterating the bus station momentarily and filling her head with exploding geometrical shapes. "Okay, listen," she said. "Tell me about the Bill Houston you know. Sounds kind of like the one I know. I'd appreciate it. Okay?"

"I just told you about him," the man said, turning the dial on a machine and grabbing the gum that dropped into its metal trough. "I see him uptown all the time. He's not a good character for you to be hanging around with. He charms the women, but when he drinks, he goes into a whole different personality." He handed the gum to Miranda and fed the machine another coin. "That the one?"

"That's him! Shit, I don't believe this. Hey," she said to Baby Ellen, who was unconscious, "he knows your Uncle Bill."

"I couldn't tell you where he is, though."

"Well, where would you guess?"

"Might be in Rheba's. Might be anywhere uptown. Might be over into like the hippy area. He wanders all over. That's the kind of guy he is."

"Yeah. Okay, well, how can I find him? Listen, I just came a long ways. I got some things to say to him."

"Do you have any change? I could call a few places maybe. They know me around here, I'm telling you. If I just ask, they'll tell me. They know I'm not out to hassle anybody. Hey—wait a minute," he said suddenly. "What if he doesn't want you to find him?"

"I'll find him anyway," Jamie said.

"Oh." He looked at Jamie, at Miranda, at the baby. "Well, I just hope this isn't a whole situation. I don't want to get anyone pissed off or anything. Right this moment, all I have is friends."

"Well, that's all I am to Bill Houston, is a friend."

"You sure? You positive?"

"All I can do is tell you," Jamie said. "Either you believe it or you don't."

"Yeah." Now the man seemed in agony, biting his lower lip and glancing about as if besieged. "Okay," he said. "Do you have some change for me? What the hell. I mean, you know him, right?"

"Take a chance," Jamie said.

"Yeah. Yeah, take a chance—I'm doing a good deed, right?"

Jamie gave him a couple of dollars in coins and sat in a pay-TV chair for half an hour looking at nothing, not even herself, in the emptiness of the dark screen. Miranda fell asleep in the seat beside hers. Baby Ellen snored in Jamie's arms, and Jamie strapped her into the plastic infant carrier. It was not possible to be less conscious than Baby Ellen was at this moment. She breathed through her toothless mouth, her eyelids like two bruises laid over her vision, the sole drifting inhabitant of an infantile oblivion that Jamie found both enviable and scary.

Jamie failed to know the situation when the man began tugging her sleeve and pushing his face into hers, his wild blond hair blotting out the world; and then she realized she'd been sleeping, was now in Chicago—"I found out where he *was,*" the man said. "He was in this place uptown a half an hour ago. And the bartender says he'd bet anything he's staying somewhere in that neighborhood. It's up north of Wilson."

"So what's the deal?" Jamie said, trying to focus on the deal.

"Trouble is, I don't know the names of the places around there, so I can't find the phone numbers. We could go up there and look around, maybe leave a few messages. I don't really know what to do, to tell you the truth. I mean, what do *you* want to do?"

"Well, I don't know. My mind is just completely shut down." She looked around the bus station's upper level, seeking some indication in its sinister drabness of what her next move should be. "My neck feels like it's on fire," was all she could summon in the way of further speech.

The man, whom she was beginning to feel might be all right—he was, at this moment, in fact, her only friend in the world—placed a gentle hand on her arm. "Tell you what. Let's get some coffee. Then we can lay out all the options, and we can figure this whole thing out."

To move themselves from immediately inside the door into the coffee shop was like undertaking a safari. They sat in a booth, the man across from the three of them. The suitcase stood in the aisle, a bulwark against the Greyhound and its hasty embarkations, cold farewells, and dubious moves. Everywhere she looked it seemed to be written: *Wouldn't you like to reconsider?* Reconsider what? she wanted to know. Everything I do will be wrong. I got no idea where I get my ideas. Coffee appeared before her, and her friend reached across the small distance between them, laying two white tablets beside her cup. "Just about anywhere you go," he said, "the bus station is the *exact* center of town. In case of a nuclear attack, this bus station would be Ground Zero." He tossed two or three similar tablets into his mouth and washed them down with an evidently painful swallow of hot coffee, screwing up his face. "If we were here when World War Three started, a bomb would drop almost in this restaurant—and do you know what? We'd be *atomized and radioactive.* It wouldn't feel like dying. We'd be turned completely into particles of light. This is the center of things."

"Some center."

"I don't say it's as happy as Walt Disney. But it *is* Ground Zero."

"What are these things?" Jamie touched the pills beside her cup.

"White crosses. They're very mild. They're equal to about two cups of coffee each. Right on, down the hatch. In three minutes you'll feel wide awake. Let me know if you want any more. Do you want a donut or something?"

Jamie ate a donut. Miranda slept heavily against her, open-mouthed, perfectly motionless, and beside Miranda, Baby Ellen slept in her infant seat. It came over Jamie that she carried her younger daughter everywhere in this seat as if she were an appliance.

They considered the situation. It was beginning to look doubtful that she'd locate Bill Houston by hanging around the neighborhood where he was known to be staying. It made more sense to take a short cab ride—the red-suited hilljack would pay for it, it was no great expense, a very short ride—to his sister's apartment and just keep calling around until they had Mr. Houston, actual and solid, on the other end of a telephone line. The more she regarded the state of things, the more it seemed that her luck was running. Rather than spend a miserable number of days hunting Bill Houston without a hint of where to start, she would take up the search in the company of one of his friends—a very poor dresser, admittedly, but a person who knew the layout and believed in good deeds. And she was beginning to feel quite sharp. Getting the kids and suitcase out to the street and into a cab was no trouble. The ride was a rocket. As she got out of the cab, holding Baby Ellen in one arm and dragging Miranda onto the pavement with her free hand, she was stunned by the world. The bricks in the building before her were keen-edged and profound. Everything had a definite quality. The fuzziness of Chicago had been burned away. Mr. Redsuit was handling things with the flourish of a Fred Astaire, and had her up two or three flights of stairs, with her kids and her suitcase, in what seemed a matter of seconds.

The hallway they travelled now was carpeted with a wide strip of black rubber down its middle. The doors to the various apartments, behind which the secret interiors seemed to breathe and mutter all around them, were of flat plyboard. One, she noticed as they passed it, was sealed from without with a padlock. Another sported a red and green bordered sign:

DR. DEL RIO, PHD.
CAN SEE, IDENTIFY, &
REMOVE YOUR DEMONS.

And the door across the hall from it opened before them onto an obviously frightened woman standing in a cramped kitchen. The expression on the woman's face was confusing to Jamie, because Jamie was feeling good.

"Oh, thanks, Ned," the woman said as the four of them spilled into the place. She held a can of beer in her hand, and cuddled it to her chest. She wore a great big overcoat and a blue beret, but did not appear, actually, to be going out. Behind the stove she now backed up against, a black scorch mark fanned out across the wall, the record of a mishap involving flames.

"Jesus, Ned," she said.

"This is so temporary I don't want to waste my breath on the whole big explanation," Ned said, brushing off his red suit as if it had accumulated some foreign matter out in the streets. Jamie, still holding the baby in her arms, realized now that he wore no overcoat—just motorvated on through the winter nights, warmed by the zeal of his mission. He moved now to embrace his sister, a gesture that seemed to startle her.

From the recesses of a darker room just off the kitchen came Anne Murray's voice singing "(You Are My) Highly Prized Possession." A man wearing thick tortoise shell spectacles now appeared at the entrance to this room and leaned against the doorframe and said nothing.

"We're going to be here about three-quarters of an hour," Ned said. "We're just going to use the phone awhile. Okay?"

"The phone doesn't work," his sister said. "They cut the phone off. You know that." She looked at the wordless man, from whose fingers dangled a bottle of beer by its neck. "He knew that two days ago," she said to him.

"Of course I know that," Ned said. "We'd just like you to look after the kids for forty-five minutes, while we make a few calls down at my place."

"What do you mean?" His sister appeared more than agitated. She had a wild, phosphorescent tension about her that brightened the whole kitchen. "You don't *have* a phone."

"Of course I have a telephone," Ned said, smiling at her. He smiled also at the other man, who raised his beer and took a pull without altering the cast of his features.

The sister seemed more alarmed by this news than by anything else Ned might have told her. "Shit," she said. "Jesus Christ. Jesus Christ."

Ned addressed the other man. "Was she about to go somewhere?"

"I think she's feeling a little chilly," the man said.

"Can you all watch these kids for a little while?"

"Guess so," the man said.

"You might even join us for a bit. You might be able to help us," Ned said. "This is Jamie. And Miranda Sue, hiding behind her mom. And here we have little three-month-old Ellen. Ellen got a middle name, Jamie?" He was holding out to Jamie the flat palm of his hand, on which lay two red capsules.

There were taking place here one or two more things than Jamie could successfully process at a single time. "What?" she said. "What are those? And who are these people?" The whole situation began flashing with a dry potent unreality.

"I was just asking after Ellen's middle name, because I was curious. And I was also offering you something to take the edge off. And this is my sister, Jean, and her husband, Randall. And these are two reds. Those white crosses, they always make me feel jumpy a little while after I eat a couple. What about you?"

"Yeah. I'm a little jumpy, I guess." Jamie accepted the two reds. "Just for a second there, I was feeling like the whole room was getting kind of yellow and zig-zaggy." Ned handed her a bottle of beer from the refrigerator, and she washed the pills down with a swallow. "Know what I mean?"

"Definitely. Yellow and zigzaggy. That means it's time to take the edge off, smooth the whole deal out, sort of. How about you, beautiful?" He offered one red pill to Jean while looking at his brother-in-law for permission. The brother-in-law nodded, and the sister swallowed it rapidly and with an air of furious resignation. Jamie could feel a liquid warm front moving in on the raw borders of her own disquiet. The room began to get slow.

Ned's apartment was on the next floor below, the hallway of which lacked but one or two functioning electric bulbs. He fiddled with his keys in the door, entertaining her with a string of chatter to which she found it unnecessary to pay any heed. "Hey," she said suddenly, watching him manipulate his key in the lock, "how about that?" On several of his fingers, Ned sported the garish flaking rings, the secret decoder jewelry of nickel gumball machines.

He opened the door onto an interior that pulsed with black-light. Dayglo posters shimmered violently on every wall. His suit was now absolutely invisible, and his hands and head seemed to drift in the air. She followed him into this weirdness. "Your name's Ned, huh?"

He shut the door behind them. In the ultra-violet his face appeared deeply tanned, the whites of his eyes now tinged with a faint blue life, like shark's meat. "My name is Higher-and-Higher," he said.

.   .   .

"Do you know about Linda Lovelace?" was the big question on
Ned Higher-and-Higher's mind. "Can you do like Linda Lovelace?" He wasn't slapping her hard, it just seemed he was trying
to keep her conscious. The brother-in-law Randall was helping.
"This is so beautiful I can't stand it," Ned Higher-and-Higher
said. The brother-in-law was quieter. He just kept doing things to
her that were rough and hard, one after another, yanking her up
by the handcuffs. She accepted that he was evil and that at the
very least, he would break her arms. She let them do everything
with a ceaseless nausea that could scarcely scratch its name on the
barbiturate serenity she inhabited. "Oh man—oh yeah—oh man
—oh yeah," Ned Higher-and-Higher said. Jamie was drifting
along the halls outside, worrying about her children. Now she was
worrying about Jamie, who was inside one of these rooms, screaming into the palm of a man's hand. She would have liked to bang
on the door here, but she was a ghost without a fist. In the dim
illumination of the hallway, the true color of the plywood was not
revealed—it might have been grey, or white, or blue. Within,
incoherent voices conspired beneath pounding rock and roll. She
witnessed the flaming communication on the door across the hall:

Madame Kay
Gifted from GOD with ESP
READER AND ADVISOR.

We are in Hillbilly Heaven, she heard herself say out loud, and
then she began to vomit as the brother-in-law started in on her
from behind. Directly before her face, one of the Seven Dwarfs
loomed up dayglo on the wall, brandishing a middle finger.

The brother-in-law wanted to do something with a knife. Ned
Higher-and-Higher, wearing the dress cap of an officer in the
United States Marine Corps, was trying to calm him down. He
was talking and talking, faster than anyone had ever spoken in

Jamie's presence. I need a cup of coffee, Jamie thought. Keep that person away from me. I'm talking about my kids, my kids. Okay; you can even do things with the knife. I just want to live through this. I just want to take care of my kids. She clocked the brother-in-law's knife with an eye as bland and dead as a camera's. There it is, she thought. The whole answer is right there in his hand.

I want you to know, her heart said to the room, that I will do anything to see my children spared.

Something came around from behind Randall and slammed into the side of his head, and he sat down on the floor against the wall with his legs sticking out like a teddy bear's. "What for?" he said. "What for?" Ned Higher-and-Higher was standing there in his Marine hat with a desk-lamp dangling from his hand. "You are the dumbest fuck," he told his brother-in-law. Randall started to cry. "This is the *last* time," Ned Higher-and-Higher told him. Okay, Jamie thought, we've crossed that one. We've gotten past the knife. Things have changed.

She was on her back with her hands cuffed behind her, her knees locked under her chin by the ongoing adrenaline convulsion of fear. Peripherally she understood that nobody human was messing with her like this, but something much more dangerous, a dark configuration of people and events, something original, something about to be named. She saw that it required what was left of her, and she felt able to meet its requirements. For the sake of her children, she found its name. She begged and begged and begged. She traded away her soul.

"What we have here is a case of fate. Of pure, dumb luck." At the very instant the dealer was offering this conclusion, Bill Houston was peeking at enough of the card beneath his ten of clubs to see that it was a diamond ace.

"Ace and a ten count as blackjack in here?" he asked.

"Are you serious? Is this guy serious?" There were tears in the dealer's eyes, and for two heartbeats Bill Houston experienced for him a searing pity. The dealer was bankrolling his own operation; this was not Las Vegas.

The restaurant the men played in was closed for business and almost entirely dark. Only the one light above them showed them the way as they laid out their bets and took their chances, glad to be among strangers.

There were four of them in the booth, and two men sitting in chairs. "What's that—five in a row?" somebody said. The others around him reacted appropriately to Bill Houston's good fortune or failed to react, according to each one's interest in his own hand. Bill Houston was betting thirty dollars at a shot right now, but in a minute the man dealing, a young fellow wearing a shabby hat for luck, would have to lower his limit owing to a lack of funds. Bill Houston warred successfully against the urge to count his money, while his heart rushed among accumulating numbers. The young man with the hat tossed him three twenties, made his other payments and collections, and threw down another round of cards. "Limit's fifteen," he said blackly to Houston. "Okay, this go-round I'm handing everybody shit." He gave them their up-cards. Bill Houston took back his thirty dollars and laid out a ten and a five. He showed a queen, and there were chuckles. "It just all depends, don't it?" the dealer said. He presented a jovial face, but it was clear he was deeply angry.

Miranda was overjoyed to be sitting in the cab's front seat. "Mama, what do these numbers say?" "Keep your hands off the meter, honey," the driver told her. "I thought I died," Jamie said, talking to Baby Ellen in her lap. Ned Higher-and-Higher kept reaching up under her skirt to squeeze her bare thigh. Jamie pushed her face against the freezing window, and that was as far away from him as she could go. "You know something?" Ned said to the cab driver, "I've seen you before. Where have I seen you?" "Just keep the kid in her seat," the driver said, "what do you want to put a little kid up front for?" "Hey, if you don't like it, we can stop right now," Ned Higher-and-Higher said. *"Ma*-ma, what do these *num*bers say? Is this a little TV scream?" Miranda said. Ned Higher-and-Higher started laughing. "Aaaaah, *shit,"* the cab driver remarked to nobody. Jamie could not stop weeping and weeping. "Loosen up," Ned Higher-and-Higher said. "It's not like you're a virgin, is it? I'm just a seducer, that's all. I'm just a destroyer. You know something?" he said, pinching her thigh and then making his fingers walk around on Baby Ellen's head, "I never met your boyfriend. I mean, *every*body has a tattoo, right? *Every*body drinks. Ha ha ha!" He leaned forward, arms draped over the front seat. "Was it in the Baghdad Lounge? Used to be the Thief of Baghdad? Do you ever go there?" When the driver failed to answer, he sat back. "I *know* I've seen you," he said. To Jamie he said: "I really fooled you, didn't I?" Out in the world, the streets whirled around them like the blades of a fan. "You have to admit," he said, "I can really charm the ladies."

When the cab stopped, he took her chin in both his hands. "Now, we're going to go in there and get you a room. You're going to go in that room and stay there all night and *don't leave.* You shut up!" he said suddenly to the driver. And to Jamie: "All right. Let's go."

She stood in a hallway while he rang bells and talked to people she didn't see. Miranda tried to put her arms around her mother's legs and go to sleep standing up, but Jamie said, "Don't touch me."

"This way," Ned Higher-and-Higher said.

They were standing in front of a door. At the end of the hall another door stood open, and beyond, a greying bathtub with the paws of an animal. Then they were standing in a room, and

Miranda was lying down on the bed. "Where's the seat? The infant seat for Ellen?" Jamie said.

"The hell with it. Put her on the bed," Ned Higher-and-Higher told her, and she put the baby on the bed immediately.

He took hold of her right hand and wrapped her fingers around some money and stood looking intently into her eyes. She wondered what was going to happen. "Do not leave this room until morning," he said, "do you understand? Do *not* leave." She nodded. Part of the room was getting closer, and part was getting unimaginably far away. "Maybe we could get together again," he said, "huh?"

Jamie sat on the bed.

"You mad?" Ned Higher-and-Higher said. "Hey—you mad?"

She studied her hand. Things were out of reach. Her legs seemed to end at the knees. "Me?" she said.

This is me.

He was gone. On the bed were her two children, and in her hand were two ten-dollar bills. This is me. Did you get what you wanted? Because I gave you everything.

This is me this is me this is me.

I have drifted, Bill Houston told himself, out of my league. Everybody's got a foreign accent. Fruits and vegetables are for sale.

He had wandered all the way up to Howard, the line between Chicago and Evanston. The Chicago side of the street was littered with small taverns and package stores, while the Evanston side, where liquor establishments were forbidden, offered vacant lots and the struggling concerns of inconsequential merchants. He stood at a newsstand and read the caption beneath the photo of a woman who looked just like Jamie: Search for Friends Ends in Tragedy. "Twenny cents," the newsguy said, as if calling out some kind of destination.

"Jesus Christ," Bill Houston said, "I don't believe it. I *know* her." He was lost. "They *raped* her."

"C'mon," the newsguy said. In his hunting cap and bulky plaid coat, he looked to Bill Houston like a moron somebody had dressed up to take into the woods; and Houston stood for a moment at the edge of violence, looking him over. He reached into the pocket of his surplus army coat, and very carefully handed the man a quarter.

They were vacuuming the Crown & Anchor in the afternoon. Through two windows on the street side, you could tell the day was turning sunny. There was no one but a couple of out-of-work substitute teachers in there, and Bill Houston, and the bartender running his machine back and forth across the defeated rug. "Teachers?" Bill Houston said. "Maybe you could teach me a few things," and the women laughed. I don't know why they respond to me, he thought; I have to look puked-on. "If you could give me some change," he said to the bartender. The bartender acted like he didn't hear, and Houston went over close and said, "Don't act like you don't hear." The bartender was not a big man. He silenced the puling of his machine by prodding it with the toe of his boot, and went inside the horseshoe-shaped bar and worked the register. Bill Houston handed him a twenty and said, "Give it to me in quarters. I got business."

Standing at the pinball machine by the payphone near the restrooms, he cracked open his roll of quarters and dropped one down the slot. It was one of the new machines that go blip blip toot toot. Stupid. Okay. In rapid succession he shot his three chances, paying the progress of each metal ball no mind whatever, and studied the contraption's face—a space-age tableau of the rock group Styx, the lead guitarist of whom was evidently about to be fellated by a mindless jungle woman strewn before his feet.

Behind them, intergalactic bodies flashed with electricity, the phosphorus-fires of infinite patience. Essentially you could never defeat these things, because they were the living dead. He moved his operation over to the telephone, dialled the number and deposited the money and said, "Mom."

The two substitute teachers were merry souls. They had taken to throwing ice at one another, giggling, chewing up their skinny red plastic straws. Mournfully indicating the ice cubes on his rug, the bartender reprimanded them. They found the idea of the rug hilarious. "Where's James, Ma?" Bill Houston said into the phone. "I'm looking for James." The teachers wanted another round, and the bartender tried to talk them into beer. Bill Houston dialled and deposited. The teachers were entertained by the suggestion that they might enjoy a beer now, and countered by suggesting that the bartender engage in solo sexual maneuvers while freshening their drinks. "James?" Bill Houston said into the telephone, "You recognize who this is?" He regarded, through clear eyes, the glittering dust that fell through the sun onto the heads of the two women and the man behind the bar. The atmosphere was muted, rarefied, and holy. "James, I'll tell you straight out," he told his half-brother, "I'm looking for some shit to get into." Completely expressionless, the bartender stood before the howling blender, grinding up for his exhilarated patrons another couple of margaritas.

Somebody at the *Tribune* told Bill Houston to call the police, and the police instructed him to get in touch with the federal Welfare. "It's me she was looking for," he explained over and over, and everyone was helpful when they learned the papers had a line on the situation. He found her at the Children's Services Division in the afternoon, napping in a chair of torn-and-taped imitation leather. Baby Ellen lay in her lap, and a few chairs away Miranda disputed with a little baldheaded boy about the possession of a coloring book. The place smelled like an ashtray. Everybody was black or foreign or deformed. There were people with crutches and people clutching soiled magazines to their chests, and children all around them. He leaned close and said, "Jamie," hoping he was being quiet enough.

When she opened her eyes she said, "I been looking for you."

"Well, you found me. How about us getting out of here?"

"I got to fill out some more forms, I think." She looked around, apparently trying to locate herself among these others.

"Shit. Once they start you on filling out forms, it just don't ever end." He tried to think of a way of explaining to her that even now, as the two of them dawdled here, these people were inventing the forms that would defeat her grandchildren.

"Miranda? Look who's here." Jamie stretched out her hand and opened and closed her fist as if trying to grab her daughter's attention. To Bill Houston she said, "Let me get my bearings, okay?"

"Get your bearings out in the world. There's no bearings in here, I guarantee you."

"Hey—I ain't ashamed," she said. "Half my goddamn family's on Welfare."

Bill Houston was exasperated. "You were looking for me, weren't you?"

"I had a few words to say to you." She was gathering up her coat, her kid's coat, her two kids. Bill Houston watched her closely, trying to determine if she was crippled in the heart. As she laid the baby where she'd just been sitting and helped Miranda get into her coat, she seemed able to concentrate through one eye only, while the other roamed a dreamland. He felt anxious and useless. "I got a suitcase around here," Jamie said.

"Excuse me," she said to the security woman behind the desk, "whatever happened to my suitcase? I got about fifteen bucks, too," she remarked to Bill Houston. "I been making money hand over fist in this town."

He was taking it as easy as he could. All through Tuesday and Wednesday Jamie was a little too quiet, and then he had to get a sitter and keep her away from the kids almost all of Thursday, because suddenly she was angrier than she knew how to handle. Her favorite movie—*Endless Love*—was playing one El stop down from their hotel, but they had to walk out of it in the middle because of the noisy conversation they were having in the dark theater. "You mean those monsters pull their shit on me and just keep on living?" She was crying out in front of the Biograph. "That the way it works? That the way it works?"

Bill Houston handed her his red bandana. "Was there something that works some other way?" He was totally sincere in asking this.

"For God's sake, listen, Bill—they went up under my skirt!"

"I know. I know. I know. But goddamn it. You step out on Clark after sundown, that whole street's going to go up under your skirt. What am I supposed to do?"

"Help me stomp their heads down to nothing! Let's kill those fuckers!"

"That's what I'd have to do," he said. "Ain't nothing short of that going to make it all right. Don't you see?"

"Then let's do it! They deserve it!"

"Shit—" a whole lot of reasons choked his speech.

"We could find them. I know we could find them. They deserve it!" Bitterly she wept.

"No way," Bill Houston said flatly. "I never murdered anybody in my life. I've done everything else but that, I guess."

"Why not?" She was clearly helpless to understand.

"I don't *know* why not! I just know this: there's something fucked up about it."

Jamie stood jamming his bandana against her nose and looking around her. "This is so real I can taste my own tongue in my own mouth." It was nearly five; the light was leaving the streets. "You know what? I've read about this place." They were standing in the alley where John Dillinger had been killed.

"What did he get?" Miranda said, putting her hands on the table and leaning over to look at Bill Houston's meal.

"Sit back down, you little weirdo," Bill ordered. "I got a bacon-cheeseburger and fries."

"He got *french* fries. That's what *I* wanted," Miranda said.

"Then you should've said so. State your wishes at the outset, otherwise you're screwed." He took a big bite.

"How do you like that?" Jamie said. "She's drinking it!" She had put Coca-Cola in the baby's bottle.

"Must be thirsty," Bill Houston said.

"I need ketchup. I need ketchup for my fries. Can I have some french fries?"

Bill Houston looked at Miranda with violence on his face. "Damn!" He got up and went over to the counter. "One small order of french fries," he told the boy. They were the only customers in the establishment, and so the boy hustled to fill the order, rocketing around in his very own fast-food universe, a tiny world half machinery and half meat.

Back at their table, Bill Houston tossed down the bag of fries for Miranda. "Open me up a ketchup, Mama," she said, and her mother told her please, and she said, "Please please please please please." A bright-faced wino at the window began to engage her in an exchange of delighted meaningless gestures. Jamie was reaching for the last packet of ketchup when Bill Houston suddenly caught her hand in his. She was irritated, thinking he meant to take it from her for his own hamburger. "Two reasons I wouldn't waste those guys," he said.

She watched him closely.

"One, I just don't want to cross that line. I don't know what's on the other side of it. You got any idea what I'm saying?"

"Sure."

"Second: I don't think it would fix anything."

"How do you know?" She wasn't combative, only curious.

"I knew guys in the joint who did away with people. They never said nothing, but you could get the idea—hey, there was this one, I *know* it didn't make him feel any better. He just wished he could do it again. Killed his wife's boyfriend."

Jamie shrugged and took a small bite of her hamburger.

"I mean, you won't stop hating them until you stop hating them."

She reached to her left and slapped Miranda's hand. "Eat like a goddamn human for once. Wipe your hands now, and start over. You know what?" she said to Bill Houston. "You're good."

"I'm just saying what I think," he answered, but he was pleased. Then he felt bad, because he wasn't good.

"Also," he said to her later on the street, "I love you."

Jamie looked him over. He was crimson-eyed and abused, but he was sober. In his awkward arms he held her infant daughter. She tried to feel uninterested, but all she could feel was saved. "What do you love *me* for, all of a sudden?" She looked up the street pointlessly.

Bill Houston couldn't explain. "I guess because you came a long ways or something. You know, to find me."

"And plus I got myself raped."

He opened up his mouth to deny it, but instead said, "That's part of it. I got to admit that, I guess."

She started to adjust the buttoning of Miranda's coat, looking at him sideways. "Well, you're not exactly Martin Hewitt, but I guess you're my Endless Love."

"Jesus. I can't take all this violin music," he said.

They started calling it The Rape, and it came to stand for everything: for coming together while falling apart; for loving each other and hating everybody else; for moving at a breakneck speed while getting nowhere; for freezing in the streets and melting in the rooms of love. The Rape was major and useless, like a knife stuck in the midst of things. They could hate it and arrange their picture of themselves around it.

When they made love, Jamie behaved quietly all through the act, as if waiting for some kind of bad news. Aroused by the mystery of her violated presence, Bill Houston couldn't stay away from her, but immediately as they were finished he would sit up and put his feet on the floor, edgy and confused, feeling like an accessory. "Look at your hands," Jamie said to him. "Look how yellow these two fingers are." She took his hand. "You're using up them Camels like you mean to die of smoking."

Bill Houston found this remark the very occasion for lighting a cigaret. He dropped the match and shoved it under the bed with his toe. "I been in touch with some people in Phoenix," he said.

"Phoenix? Like in Phoenix, Arizona?"

"Some bad people," he said.

Her stomach grabbed. "Phoenix, Arizona, USA?" She took a puff from his cigaret herself. "What do you have in mind?"

"Well," he said, "I don't know. Maybe nothing. I just thought we'd go to Phoenix, is all."

"But who are these people you're in touch with? These bad people."

"Friends and relations," Bill Houston said.

3

It was past noon, but the house still kept some of the chill of night. In its cool dark Mrs. Houston read her Bible and listened to KQYT very low. Neither shall he multiply wives unto himself, that his heart not turn away: neither shall he greatly multiply to himself silver and gold, Deut. 17:17. These laws ought to have been clearly understood by the Mormons to the east of her, and by the rich to the north. The page's heading read ALL IDOLATROUS MUST BE SLAIN.

The mailbox clanked, and she drew aside the curtain one inch and looked out into the heat. The mailman, dressed in shorts and wearing a pith helmet, was just leaving her territory. Mrs. Houston went to the closet to get some protection from the sun.

Wearing an enormous straw hat, she stepped out into the yard.

The yard was dirt. Near the front of the house, but out of its shade, a mesquite bush collapsed away from its own center, ashimmer in the afternoon and appearing on the brink of bursting into flames. One small purple cactus and a thriving cholla about three feet high—wrapped in a cottony haze that was, in fact, composed of innumerable small vicious barbs—stood up between two junked Ford sedans circa the fifties. She kept the cars because she believed that one day from these two heaps of rubbish her sons would build her a functioning automobile. Her sons would do this because they all three loved cars and understood their workings, and because they owed her. They owed her the courtesy of their obedience and the devotion of their labors. They were a generation of torment, and they owed her.

One brown federal envelope lay unaccompanied in her mailbox. This monthly allotment of Social Security, along with whatever she could garner from the occasional sale of pastries, was her livelihood. She would go to the bank now, drawing the bulk of her check in cash, which she secreted among her underthings in the bureau drawers, and putting aside twenty-seven fifty in her savings account. She didn't know what amount she might have saved over the years—she was careful never to examine her bank book. She had never touched her savings. She had important plans for it: plans involving the End of Times, and the Desolation of Abomination.

The neighborhood was almost entirely Mexican, and as she walked out into its post-meridian hush, she spat in the street. Among these houses of flimsy wood, their interiors dark and, like hers, already beginning to smolder with the obliterating summer, she felt strangled by a jungle Catholicism that she knew to be superstitious, diabolical, and mesmerized by sex. She might have put it that she had nothing against her neighbors; it was just everything connected with them.

All around her were the people who would thwart her. Some

of the houses attempted to look pink, or green, but most seemed never to have been painted, only constructed out of scrap and expected to return to it soon. Just a couple of blocks west, warehouses and shut factories began to shoulder in among the dwellings. The Phoenix Sky Harbor lay to the south and east: periodically her thinking was driven down into itself by the passing of a jet plane just overhead, a searing presence of which she was no longer ever consciously aware. Mormons farther on—filthy rich to the north—percolating black snakehandlers to the south. As Phoenix's daily temperature increased, boiling them all alive, she experienced herself in its stunning brightness as a woman under siege.

She stood in the street, preparing to go to the bank, and something she had just been reading swept over her. The hands of the witnesses shall be first upon him to put him to death, and afterward the hands of all the people. So thou shalt put the evil away from among you, Deut. 17:7. These laws ought to have been clearly understood by the multitudes.

Her bank was the First State, one of three identically constructed branches serving east, west, and central Phoenix. In the grandness of its style, it had the air of an arboretum—she always expected to see some birds aloft in the reaches of its gigantic plants. A security guard manned a centrally located information desk. Everything was made of attempted marble. Mrs. Houston admired the cool surfaces on which she wrote her deposit slip and leaned waiting for the line of people to clear, and she admired also the security guard, a tanned gentleman with silver hair. He seemed to have sprung unsullied into this refrigeration and light, like Adam. She made a point of going near him as she approached the line for the tellers' windows, and she stopped a minute to pass the time of day. "You have an aura of holiness," she said. He smiled a bland and careful smile. "Auras are visible to me in the hot months of the spring," she informed him. "Signs and tangents manifest themselves to me."

Suddenly she was terrified to have made this admission—but he seemed a man of such kindness, prepared to receive any news with a friendly neutrality and a slight nod of the head, like one gone deaf. But he wasn't deaf. "Do you have some business inside this bank, Ma'am?" he said.

"Of course I do," Mrs. Houston answered. "Don't you know me?"

He made a face of weary apology. "I probably see five hundred people—"

"I've been here fifty times or more," she interrupted. "Every first of the month."

He shook his head, and the sadness with which he did it made her sad. "You don't know me," she said, and moved in some confusion into the tellers' line. It wasn't that she expected to be known by all the bank's employees; it was just that she had been lovely once, and had never really believed that time would make her faceless.

For a second, standing in line behind a half dozen people, she felt as if no one part of her was connected to any other. At times like this her stomach made a fist, and she saw that it was useless to cry out to the Lord.

Mrs. Houston walked seven blocks toward the low humps of South Mountain. It was hot. Whenever she glanced toward the sun inadvertently, it turned black upon her retinae. Down by Carter Street she turned in at the doorway of the only three-storey building for blocks.

At the bottom of the stairs inside, she paused and collected her strength—not that she was frail, or that the stairs were arduous;

but she had no idea what might await her, what might be foretold, in Rosa's Cantina. In a minute she began to climb, passing the second floor with its closed tattoo parlor, its second-hand record shop and its Chicano drug rehabilitation office. On the third floor, having paused to pray Dear God let it be true and happy, she entered the permanent cool opium moment of Rosa's.

It was an afternoon of slow business. Around most of the half dozen collapsible card tables, folding chairs painted a brilliant enamel purple waited empty. The floor was linoleum, the wall spangled with the glued-on six-inch silhouette cut-outs of guitars and mariachis and G and Treble clefs, an interior decorating touch retained, like the name "Rosa's," from an earlier time when the place had actually been some kind of cantina. As she entered, wishing she could be told which table was absolutely the right one for this afternoon, Mr. Carlson hurried out of nowhere to guide her—a tall man with a bald head and a pathetic toupee he sported ostentatiously, like a hat. Mrs. Houston made no resistance as he steered her by her elbow to the table precisely in the center of the room, equidistant between the portraits, on either facing wall, of a grave and beautiful dancing girl in a red gown, and a young toreador in his *traje de luces*—his suit of lights.

She let herself breathe easy. The air seemed cooler than in fact it was, because the late sun was filtered through curtains that were gauzy and white. Two tiny air conditioners laid a mild pale noise along the air, rendering almost inaudible the Latin disco issuing from automotive stereo speakers placed on a windowsill. Mr. Carlson brought her some black tea in a cup stamped with the logo of Thomas's Cafeteria.

At the only other occupied table, Mr. Miguel Michelangelo entertained a group of three young Chicana girls with a humorous reading of the Tarot cards. The girls were satisfying some curiosity and brought only discord into Mrs. Houston's afternoon, having no appreciation of the state of things. Staring at her cup, she held back a moment before letting herself take a sip of her tea. She herself approached these occasions seriously, with the purpose of gaining some knowledge of her sons, the three of whom were harassed, plagued, and intermittently controlled by the Evil One.

Miss Sybil, who had been sitting quietly by the window, who had in fact been staring minutely at the curtain as if looking out into a world of white meaning, now recognized Mrs. Houston's presence and glided over and sat down. Miss Sybil waited politely and wordlessly with her hands folded, a Jewish lady from Queens, the outline of whose monstrous brassiere showed plainly through her sheer yellow blouse. When Mrs. Houston had drunk half her tea, Miss Sybil lifted her cup and began stirring the leaves, dragging them up the sides of the cup with the spoon. "I see you making progress," she said. "I see you suffering a setback. I see you going forwards and backwards but I see you only going backwards a little, I see you going mostly forward into the future. You got children? I see children, I see boys—boys? How many? Three? And do I see how many girls—two, one? No girls, okay. Any boys living at home still? That's right, I see one who almost lives at home—comes to visit a lot. The youngest?" She paused for breath, stirring the leaves. Mrs. Houston felt a vague annoyance that Miss Sybil seemed never to remember anything about her, but always had to rediscover everything in the tea leaves— prompted, Mrs. Houston knew, by her own involuntary answers to the questions Miss Sybil asked. "What's this?" Miss Sybil asked now, and went silent again. The hum of the air conditioners evened everything out; the atmosphere was without a ruffle. "I see you're very concerned about something—something—some-thing . . ."

"William Junior, my oldest boy—what do you see?"

"I see the oldest boy, the oldest boy—he's not in town now? No, doesn't live here anymore—you gonna see him pretty soon? Maybe?"

Mrs. Houston gripped the woman's wrist. "When?"

She shook herself free. "Pretty soon, I think—maybe pretty soon, maybe not for a long time. Maybe in a few days."

"Has some kind of evil got my boy?"

Miss Sybil put down the teacup. Beneath their exotic make-up, her eyes were simple—beady, and vexed by the visible world. "Evil?" She had two sons of her own. She had emigrated from Queens eleven years before. "What, exactly?—evil." She regarded the elderly lady across the table from her—the tense mother, unshakeably hillbilly. It required no scrutiny of leaves to know the kind of existence that lay behind her and ahead of her, a life very much like the life of Miss Sybil, who blinked twice, looking at Mrs. Houston, and said, "Yes. The Evil has him."

Mrs. Houston was confused by the definiteness. "But won't...?" She trailed off, her speechlessness blending with the white voices of the air conditioners.

"Won't what?" Miss Sybil looked at her own palm.

Mrs. Houston gripped her by the wrist again, almost violently. "Won't the good triumph? You always see the good in things. You always say in the end—"

"That's in the future," Miss Sybil said irritably. "It's easy to talk about the future being so good and all, because it never comes, dear. But all you gotta do is look around you for half a minute. Nobody's keeping it a secret from us that we're all in the toilet. We're in the sewer. Forecast tomorrow is more of the same. Don't tip me, darling, I don't want your money." She stood up abruptly, a motion that attracted the attention of Mr. Miguel Michelangelo and the three young ladies. "You're too unlucky." She disappeared with the teacup into the little kitchen.

Mrs. Houston sat at the table a minute, flushed and enervated, against her will, by the prospect of a terrible future.

A complex rataplan of bongos and piano made itself heard amid her thoughts, and she became aware of a young Chicano in a tan suit adjusting the dials of the stereo. He sat down at the table nearest the two speakers where the cool light fell upon him, and he made it seem the appointed table. He projected, in Mrs. Houston's sight, a riveting mystical presence. She did not want to go near him.

"*Corazon—hai! hai!—corazon,*" low voices cried from the speakers. The boy—no older than sixteen, probably—began talking to himself, looking at nobody. Clearly he'd put himself almost instantly into some manner of trance. Feeling like a violator, Mrs. Houston stared at him. He wasn't beautiful, but had a kemptness about him that looked as if it might have been painful to maintain. His lips, moving together and parting swiftly, independent of his stony other features, were red as a doll's. She couldn't hear what he was saying—he was scarcely even whispering now—but she thought she caught the word "murder" or "martyr" and another that sounded like "serious" or "series." She wondered if he could be speaking English. She had never before seen an entranced individual. She drew near him now because she had to.

Careful to make no disturbance moving the chair, she sat down next to him. He stared forward, his black pupils turned upward just a couple of degrees. Before him on the table, the fingers of his two hands interlocked whitely. "The void of the Saints drugged in the deeds of the past," he whispered without inflection or tone. "The belief and the agony groans of eyelets. Many small eyelets that see many things."

Mrs. Houston concentrated on the image in her mind's eye of her son William, and she laid two dollars near the boy's convulsive hands. She put out of her mind the idea that he might be faking. She understood nothing; but she believed the answers were here.

"The seeking of things in outer space," the boy was saying, "things lost to us, things coming back, things going away into the void of the eye. Every face is a moment, every moment is a word, every word is yes, every yes is now, every now is a vision of belief."

Although his eyes weren't closed, they suddenly gave her the impression of having opened. "Was there anything to interpret?" he said. "Perhaps you heard something worth pondering. I don't know." He didn't touch the money. Mrs. Houston was silent, trying to recall and commit to memory the whispered words of his prophecy. Face is moment is word is yes is now—every now is a vision of belief. She knew what "yes" meant: William Junior. Yes, he was coming to Phoenix. The rest she would have to ponder, just as this seer had indicated.

She grew unquiet under his gentle gaze. She wanted to say something that might get him to go away. She made a gesture toward the two dollars on the table between them. "Please talk to me about yourself," he said. "Just for a few minutes, and then I have to go."

His interest was so clearly genuine that it alarmed her. "Well, what would I want to talk about?" Her heart began to race. "All of a sudden I feel shy as a girl. But I ain't one," she said— remembering the guard's indifference at the bank. "I'll be seventy the next first of August, God willing."

She stopped talking; but the boy didn't stop looking at her face. He didn't seem prying, or even all that curious. He was only there; he was merely interested.

"I like to listen to the KQYT," she ventured. "You know—the station where they never have any talking? I play it real low, like it's hardly there. A girl in the checkout told me, I was at the Bayless's, said I ought to go back up into the hills, if I didn't care for those prices. Well, I'm here to tell you, I live on a fixed income. I got to complain about these prices, don't I? *Some*body's —we *all* got to complain and cry out for the President to show mercy. And I ain't nobody from the hills, if it comes down to that. I'm a red-dirt woman from the dead middle of Oklahoma. You'll see a slope in that land ever now and then, but never one single hill, I promise you. I worry about my boys, because they're fallen.

Two been to prison, and my youngest is mixed up in his brains
—he'll go too, before I pass on. I'll live to see him suffer the
darkness of a prison like the other two. William Junior is my
first-born, fathered by my first husband, my real husband. James
and Burris come out of the loins of Harold Carter Sandover. I'm
not ashamed I never married him—I mean to tell you, *he* never
married *me,* is all. He talked the slick way, the way that makes
a woman believe a man—gets you imagining you must've married
him yesterday, and then forgot all about it. Oh, he could turn out
the light and put a movie in the air with words. Talked himself
right into Florence Prison, into the Cellblock Six, the Super Max.
He'll never, never get out, and I can't go visit and be any kind
of help to him, or nothing. His own fault! Who would've married
him in a second? Who said he'd marry her tomorrow but never
did? They said he'd be away for two to five, but he got himself
in some kind of a jackpot down there, they call it, with some of
the men supposed to be guarding them all from escape. Then he
moved over the walls to the Maximum, and he was okay there for
a while, but a man in there got his arm shot away one night, and
a gang of them tried to convince the world it was H. C. Sandover
had a hold of that revolver when it was firing off. Then he died
—not H.C., I don't mean to say, just the man who stirred up the
trouble so that somebody had to shoot him, I guess was how the
situation went, anyway that's the news that came to me—that in
a prison you've got a code to follow or die, and this man had broke
away from the code. And they put H.C. inside the Super Max,
where nobody but your family can visit—the legal family, and the
blood. But why do they let all the reporters in there to interview
somebody like Stacey Winters? They had him in the papers last
week! It isn't fair, is it? I live by the word of our Lord Jesus Christ.
I cling to him as my rock in a storm, his teachings do I follow,
amen, amen—but I don't get the picture of it, somehow. I call
it shit, shit—I don't mind saying it, it's a word you'll find in the

Bible. Now he's in that Cellblock Six, and I can feel the evil all over my first-born son William Junior like the prickly you get on a wool sweater—" she shook her fingers and made a face, as if she'd touched something with a mild charge. "I was thirty-three years old before I ever bore a child." And suddenly she fell silent, and scratched her nose, and seemed to have forgotten she was speaking at all.

The boy left the table without saying anything. The money she had laid out for him remained. Mr. Carlson came out to turn on the fluorescent lights.

When she'd walked down the stairs and out of the building, she was surprised to see that it was nearly dark. Down the block an ambulance was stopped at the curb, emitting blue and white light. Things seemed unbelievably quiet. Children stood about scarcely speaking. The curious were silhouetted in their windows, waiting for something to transpire. Mrs. Houston felt a fist of ice in her chest, but it relaxed and was gone as she realized that this ambulance, these people, whatever tragedy the street had made, could have nothing to do with her. Men carried an aluminum stretcher by its handles out of a billiard lounge; then, as soon as the ambulance's doors slammed behind it, the noise started up, and everything began to melt away. To Mrs. Houston's ears, these modern sirens seemed to cry *we-you we-you we-you*. The bystanders disappeared. The street again put on the aspect of a place where things could only fail to occur. She looked up above her at the third-floor window: through the sheer curtain she could make out Mr. Carlson wiping off a table.

The streets were almost instantly cooler as the dark fell. The wind was starting up as it always seemed to do at this hour, raising clouds of dust and making things rattle. Mrs. Houston was trudging forward, head down, a handkerchief held over her mouth, and she nearly ran into Jeanine Phillips by the mailbox because she hadn't seen Jeanine there as she approached. Oh spare me, Mrs. Houston thought. Jeanine was carrying that big heavy blue religious book beneath her arm. "I was going to leave you a note," Jeanine said. She removed her hand from Mrs. Houston's mailbox.

"You're after my check," Mrs. Houston said. "You're just after my check."

Jeanine looked very pert this evening—something like a nurse. She wore a white raincoat, and she'd had her blond hair cut off short. "I wasn't doing anything," she insisted.

"My money's in the bank," Mrs. Houston told her.

"Can I come in and talk to you for a while? I need to talk to you about Burris."

"Won't do Burris no harm to go without his dope for one day," Mrs. Houston said.

They stood in the wind for a moment, wordless.

"Some people," Jeanine began, "their material existence is very painful for them. I know I get too crazy over Burris and I forget what the priority should be, I mean, we should help him to make it to the next highest plane, Mrs. Houston—the morontia life."

Mrs. Houston felt the air move through her as if she were made of gauze, and she shut her eyes. The tangled gnostic catechism of her youngest son's girlfriend always made her dizzy. "You tell Burris this that I'm telling you right now: my money won't buy him nothing but more suffering. He's got to learn—why"— she was suddenly overcome with passion—"this is a beautiful world! Joy is our chief purpose—"

"The *thing is,*" Jeanine interrupted. "Mrs. Houston, the thing is he can't eat, he can't sleep, he can't receive the imprint of his Thought Adjuster. Every one of us has a Thought Adjuster kind of like assigned to you. And when you're asleep—oh, I don't know how it works. He needs to sleep. Burris needs to sleep. He can't sleep."

"Tell him what he needs is to get down on the floor of his misery and *pray.*"

Jeanine let out an ugly sob that was almost like the bark of a dog. "He'll never pray!" She was standing there in the yard, carrying the big book of nonsense by which she pretended to live.

Behind her, the house was dark. Mrs. Houston tasted the dust and salt on her own lips. "Well," she said, "you want some lemonade? And I got chocolate milk, if you want that instead."

"Thank you," Jeanine said.

"But there ain't no money for Burris's dope. Just lemonade or chocolate milk, and that's the whole of it." She led the way inside.

Jeanine left before eleven. Another twenty dollars gone into nothing—and why? Because I love my son. I feel just the same this instant as when I held him in my arms and he was my baby. I was forty-five years old . . . She moved about the house dusting things with her handkerchief. For years she'd been an habituée of the nighttime talk shows, but since Christmas she'd been without TV—hers had been stolen on December 24. She didn't like to let herself think that Burris had stolen it—but who else could it have been?

Leaving the kitchen light on, she retired to her bed in the back room with her Bible. Sometimes she felt very confused to look up from the Old Testament and see her electric Timex on the chest of drawers, and then think of the world with its radar, its microwaves, the Valley Communications Building made entirely out of glass.

She let the Bible lie on her stomach and fell asleep with the light on. She dreamed of a man being shot to death.

It was Sunday.

James Houston leaned his head from the truck's passenger window and spat out saliva brought into his mouth by intense nausea. Ford Williams was driving, and Dwight Snow sat between them holding his clipboard on his lap.

"What's your problem there?" Ford asked, shouting above the wind of their passage. He steered with one hand, rubbing his eyes and exhibiting signs of nervousness with the other.

"I do not know, my friend," James said. "I think I put some shit in my body last night that my body don't like." There was a beer bottle shoved into the ruptured paneling of the door to keep it still, and some kind of artificial flower sprouted from the bottle's mouth. "Shit my body hates, in fact." He plucked the flower and smelled it, and threw it out the window. Dwight Snow said, "Hey," and then lit a cigaret.

James said a few more words nobody could hear, because his face was out the window.

They moved at seventy miles an hour into a steadily intensifying landscape. It was quarter to seven, an hour of the morning presided over by one half of a perfectly flat and orange vicious sun. Cactuses standing knee-high in the desert threw shadows fifty feet long. For dozens of miles around them, every surface was either purple or blinding. Behind and southeast of them lay Phoenix like a dream materializing out of smog. "Well," Ford Williams announced, "they say fried foods angry up the blood."

"That got something to do with something?" James asked. He could scarcely hear himself, with the wind and the rattling.

"Man, it ain't even seven AM in the fucking morning," Ford said, "so don't ask me."

"Just trying to keep track of whatever. I mean like whether we're having a real conversation or whether we're just having seven AM," James said.

Ford said, "I'm just starting to believe in this highway. Two three minutes, I'll be all of half awake." He turned his head and shouted "Coffee!" in Dwight Snow's ear. Dwight failed even to blink, drawing on his cigaret and looking straight into the highway's approach through opaque eyes that were something like a lizard's.

In a minute Dwight consulted the vehicle titles on his clipboard. "We're talking about exit fourteen," he said.

"Is that all it says?" James spat out the window again. "I like all that detail there. How we supposed to find it?"

"It's right on the road. We're talking about two motorcycles, one red Cadillac, one powder blue BMW sportscar. When we find them, there we are."

"About four miles. I'm talking about exit fourteen," Ford said.

"All that stuff supposed to go? Moto-sickles and the whole etcetera?" James asked.

"This person is a chronic overextender of his limits, huh?" Ford asked.

"Two motorcycles. One Cadillac. One BMW," Dwight repeated.

"Guy's got his own personal national debt or something," Ford said.

"We take all his shit, how's he going to get to the store for water?" James asked.

"Probably got ten other cars," Ford said. "Financed by various other outfits."

Dwight made marks on the titles with his pen as if engaged in actual business, but there was no reason whatever to mark on the titles. "Let's be thinking about how we're going to get it all," he said.

"I say we just confront him at gunpoint, and keep him absolutely still while we go after our God-appointed mission taking things," Ford said. "Like walk right in his back door."

Dwight sighed loudly enough to be heard even with the wind and the pickup's noise.

"Well it ain't like we can just sneak all that stuff *away* from him," Ford said. "Please be reasonable."

"Reasonable? You don't know the meaning of the word," Dwight said.

James clutched a used styrofoam cup to his face and vomited a little bile into it. He tried to scare Dwight by pretending to dump it in Dwight's lap, and then threw it out the window. He pounded on the glove compartment before him until it opened, and withdrew from there a great big Colt revolver.

"What are you going to do with that?" Dwight asked.

"I gone shootchoo, muh-fuckah," James said. He began firing at things out the window in the desert.

One of the motorcycles was a beautiful Harley cruiser with a windshield and saddlebags, and the other was a little Honda trailbike already ridden mercilessly into premature old age. James and Dwight easily lifted the trailbike into the back of the pickup, but the Harley they would have to fire up and load by driving it up the portable ramp, simultaneously starting the Cadillac and the BMW in order to waste no time. "This ain't going to happen in a smooth manner," Ford said. He was talking very low, his arms draped over the railing of the pickup, and his head resting on his arms, as if he'd soon fall asleep. No one seemed to have detected their presence yet. The house—just a shack, really, a couple of rooms and no more—lay in the shadow of a gigantic rock. The Cadillac was nudged up against the dwelling, directly under a window. The BMW was parked behind the Caddy, not an inch of space between them. Clearly, repossession had been anticipated. "So what's the procedure, friends?" Ford said.

"I say we go in and blow his head off, rape the females, eat his food, and burn his house." This was James's suggestion.

"We're going to proceed as per regulations," Dwight said.

"You look a little pale there, Dwight," Ford said. "You scared?"

"I don't get much sun lately," Dwight said. "Let's just proceed. I'm the BMW, you're the Caddy, James is the Harley. And obviously you get to drive the truck," he said, turning to James.

"Oh well gee I sure like that," James told him.

"If you think I gave you guys the shit detail and me the safest," Dwight said, "you're correct."

They moved to their tasks, projecting an air of cautious efficiency that bordered on dread. The sun was higher. The box canyon around them was like a spoon of light. Dwight was having a little difficulty opening the BMW's door with a coathanger. Ford had to help him when he was done with the Cadillac. Nobody talked now. James had the cover off the Harley's ignition and was laying it quietly in the back of the pickup when Dwight came over to him, furious, talking low. "Goddamn it, what's that thing in your belt? Put that in the fucking truck."

James stared at him, resting a hand on the butt of the Colt protruding from the waist of his pants. "I just like to feel in charge, Dwight."

"Well, you're not in charge—I am. I got a business here. What we're doing is legitimately repossessing merchandise for which a regular, everyday citizen has failed to pay. You insist on carrying that weapon, we're moving over into the area of robbery with aggravation."

"I don't want to get shot."

"That heat will not protect you from bullets. It will just get you fucked up with the law. We've had this little talk before, James. Get your head on, okay?"

"Fuck."

Dwight sighed. "You are no longer working for me."

James sighed, too. "Blah blah blah," he said, and went around and put the pistol on the seat of the truck.

Ford was already signalling, by his hand out the Cadillac's window, that he was ready to wire the vehicle and proceed. Dwight went over to him and said, "Did you look under the hood?"

"What's the difference?" Ford said. "Let it start or don't start. If he's got the distributors stashed, he's got them stashed, that's all. You want to move or not?"

"We don't want that one starting"— he pointed over at the BMW—"and this one failing to start. Because then we'll have noise without movement." He looked over the Cadillac's roof at the low distant hills.

Indicating by the slant of his shoulders that none of this was necessary, Ford got out of the car and as silently as possible raised its hood. Then he lowered it and got back into the car, now indicating by the slant of his shoulders that he'd been right.

"We'll give it a shot, okay," Dwight said. He got quietly into the blue BMW and wired it beneath the dash. James sat astride the Harley, hand raised aloft. Dwight raised his hand out the BMW's window.

I'm going to come, James thought. Dwight dropped his hand.

I love it, James thought. He put the wires together and the Harley fired up and he kicked it forward up the ramp. Simultaneously, smoke exploded from the pipes of the BMW and the Cadillac. James jumped off the motorcycle, letting it fall on its side in the bed of the pickup. The two cars were now moving almost in unison backward. James tossed the ramp up into the truck as if it weighed nothing and slammed the gate. Dwight was already on the road, Ford Williams immediately behind him.

From one of the windows of the house, a weapon began firing. The cars were well away from the scene, but James was still getting into the truck. Whatever the house's occupant was using indicated a serious nature and a sincere intention to commit murder—bullets chewed up the dirt and rattled with a terrifying clatter into the truck's body. A machine gun, I'm dead, James thought. He had the door open and reached over to lift the Colt from the seat. The automatic weapon had ceased for an instant, but it began again now, slamming into the side of the truck a fusillade that made it seem quite fragile. Lying across the seat, James reached the pistol out the window and fired twice. The Colt, a forty-four caliber, nearly tore his finger off, recoiling at an awkward angle. With his left hand he turned the key in the ignition. He fired twice more, hitting only the infinitely blue sky of morning, laid the pistol on the seat, and rose up to put the truck in gear. I'm dead, I'm dead, I'm dead—the acrid, brimstone smoke of cordite filled the cab now, and he couldn't breathe. Another burst of fire came from the house, but flew wide of him as the truck leapt forward. As he turned out of the yard and accelerated onto the roadway, his back throbbed violently where the flesh anticipated its wounds.

At the entrance to the freeway, the Cadillac and BMW awaited him. The three entered bumper-to-bumper doing eighty. "Convoy," James said to no one. "Fucking convoy." He heard only a tremendous black ringing in his head. Coming in behind him through the rear window, the morning sun turned the truck's interior an unbelievable gold, the gold of conquistadors, the gold of obsession and enslavement.

James was wiping his face with a bandana as he came in. His was one of the few two-storey dwellings in the neighborhood, and the kitchen, for reasons nobody could explain now, was upstairs. He was a little out of breath as he stood before the refrigerator, keeping its door ajar with one hand and fluttering the hem of his teeshirt with the other. "Don't we have any lemonade?" he asked Stevie.

She had a magazine flattened before her on the formica table. Beside it lay a pair of sewing scissors and a stack of discount coupons. "Lemonade? Seems to me like we did. Don't we?"

James popped a beer. "Where's Wyatt?"

"He's downstairs. Out back, I guess," Stevie said.

"Out back? What's he doing?"

"Leave him alone, honey."

"All's I said is what is he doing. I'm just standing here. That okay?" A shudder of elation passed through him as he looked out the window at the low roofs of houses and the flat dusty neighborhood, thinking of how the bullets had torn through the side of the pickup: and now he was standing here alive. "Okay for me to ask about my son?" Observing Stevie with her magazine and her scissors and her coupons, he experienced the same elation, a thrill of feeling as palpable and cool as the beer in his stomach, and realized that he loved his wife very much. "I love you, Stevie," he said.

In surprise she looked up at him. Her nails were long and she'd painted them red, to match her lipstick. A scarf of flowery design covered some rollers in her dark hair. "I love you too, baby," she said. She held out her hand to him, and he stepped over and took it in his own. They remained thus awkwardly for a minute, almost as if James had meant to take her pulse, and had discovered there wasn't any. "I rustled up some bedding for your brother and his touring company," she said. "We can play hospitality to the whole outfit."

His son Wyatt began screeching out by the door like a crow. "Can't he open that door by himself?" He let go his wife's hand and scratched his belly viciously.

"Maybe his hands are full," Stevie said.

"You want the door open talk English!" James shouted down

the stairs. There was a big Corning Ware pot on the stove, and suddenly he noticed that the windows were steamy near the ceiling and the walls dripped with a little moisture: she'd been cooking stew, or soup. Claustrophobia touched him. He went to the head of the stairs and saw his son at the screen door down there, wearing a green cowboy hat with a string that went under his chin, his hands dangling at his sides, screeching for assistance and pretending he didn't know how to talk or open a door. "Hey," James said. "Open up that door by yourself."

"Baby—" Stevie said, as the boy let out another yodel of feigned despair.

"He's acting like a two-year-old," James said to her, and spoke softly and clearly down the stairs: "Shut up and open that door." Wyatt kept on hollering wordlessly, kind of talking around James, James perceived, to the boy's mother—as if James weren't standing there at all. An almost uncontrollable rage gripped the father in the region of his heart. "If I have to come down those stairs, I will make you regret it forever," he told his son. Then he came down the stairs two at a time and shoved the door open violently, so that Wyatt sat down and set up a cry that was completely genuine and more than somewhat terrified. James yanked him up onto his feet by the hand and showed him the door. He was surprised to find that he was still holding his can of beer, and he took a drink from it, making a conscious effort to slow himself down. "Now you reach up and open that motherfucking door, or I will kill you," he told his son. Wyatt raised his arm and let it fall back, giving out with miserable sobs. "Don't fuck with me," James said, and turned him around and spanked him hard three times on the seat of his oversized black shorts. He put him back in front of the door. "Go, you little shit," he said. "Do not disobey me." Although Wyatt lifted his arm and took hold of the doorlatch, he seemed helpless to operate it. Convinced he was shamming, James turned him around and slapped his face back-

and-forehanded, and Wyatt fell as if struck by paralysis onto the wooden porch. His sobs carried out over the street. James stood over him with a beer in his hand.

Suddenly shame made him give up this contest of wills. He opened the screen door, dragged his son through it with one hand and deposited him there, and then stood on the porch looking across the street at the neighbors' place, feeling torn apart. He believed they were watching. He flung his beer into the roadway between him and their prying eyes, trying to find some word that might make this unexpected incident comprehensible. I have one of the very few two-storey places in this whole section of town, he told some fancied inquisitor.

He decided to go over a couple of blocks to Michael's Tavern for something cold, and as he walked beside the road he felt his anger burning up in the heat of noon, and saw himself, as he often did when he was outdoors on hot days, being forged in enormous fires for some purpose beyond his imagining. He was only walking down a street toward a barroom, and yet in his own mind he took his part in the eternity of this place. It seemed to him—it was not the first time—that he belonged in Hell, and would always find himself joyful in its midst. It seemed to him that to touch James Houston was to touch one iota of the vast grit that made the desert and hid the fires at the center of the earth.

Outside in the night the dust began to coat the surface of the water, and the styrofoam life preserver, hanging by its nylon rope, banged continually against the chain-link fence around the pool. Burris Houston concentrated on this sound, and on the sounds of things moved by the wind that found its way into the apartment through any minuscule aperture. He sat in the wicker chair in the living room, dark save for the light of a single tiny reading lamp, his knees drawn up to his chin, drinking a beer and Jack Daniels whiskey and watching the shadow of a model Japanese Zero as it moved on the wall. He was sick inside, withdrawing contrary to his will from heroin.

He tried to forget all about his body, watching the mobile shadow of the weapon of a defeated nation, sipping the liquor, listening to the repeated, nearly comprehensible signalling of the life preserver against the fence outside. He tried to concentrate on the atmosphere—the dust and plyboard aura of dwellings thrown up hastily around swimming pools in the desert. He waited, in a state beyond patience or impatience, for his woman. In his mind's eye and in the shrunken room of his heart, Jeanine came to him with money in her hand, maneuvering like a ghost of mercy down the curbless street lined with wheelless hotrod automobiles on cinderblocks.

But he didn't call Jeanine his woman in his heart. Amid a rush of good luck, intoxicants, and money, he'd been married fourteen months ago to Eileen Wade, whom he couldn't stop loving, despite the fact that he passionately hated her.

At her job at a rock-and-roll place up on MacDowell, Eileen had always worn hot-pants and stockings with seams down the calves, and he'd leaned against the bar every night going deaf from whatever band might be playing, proud to get special attention from her because she was his wife, and prouder still to think how the other men leaning against the bar—flushed and drunken cowpokes who didn't know how they'd gotten there, or empty purveyors of cocaine wearing golden rings, with necklaces waiting to be tightened around their throats—needed what he had, and couldn't get it. They needed to share one secret after another with a beautiful woman, to peel away layer after layer, mask after mask, and still find themselves worshiped.

But everything had fallen to pieces somewhere in the disordered barrooms of the city, and Eileen had turned unaccountably into someone else—all the songs on the radio talked about his experience. Eileen was living now with a man known to him only as Critter, a dealer in drugs, a person very much at the center of things, and there was talk that she was pregnant. But Burris didn't believe it. Critter had many qualities for a woman to admire, but there was something not quite right about the man, and whenever Burris let his mind run, it started to seem obvious that something was not quite right about the whole situation, and it seemed to him only temporary—as if all of this was a stupid mistake, something Eileen would regret soon. And as he considered these things, suffering the crawling of withdrawal through his ribs and chest, bathing his electrified bones in whiskey to quiet them, he became certain that Eileen regretted it already, and he realized that all he needed to do to change everything was to see her just once.

Memories assailed him of how gently she had spoken, touched, and moved; of how she'd loved him fiercely despite his mistakes and obsessions and weaknesses. And the conviction descended on him that love like theirs couldn't possibly suffer any change.

The wind was still blowing when he stepped from the apartment, and it nearly wrenched the doorknob out of his hand, but it had died down by the time he'd walked six blocks to Roosevelt Street, where he stood by the curb with his thumb out. Dust hung in the air under the streetlamps; soon the stars would burn clearly above the city. Not many cars drove past tonight—it occurred to Burris he might step inside somewhere for a drink and ask among the other customers for a ride. It amazed him how simple it all actually was: he only had to go to her and tell her he was ready, that she could come back to him now, and everything would be returned to sanity. Pride had blinded him in the past, and a pain that eluded him tonight, and an anger he didn't feel toward her anymore. Freed of negative energies, he moved easily toward solutions.

A pickup truck went past him, and in the back of it a man with his pants down stood up and pointed his naked buttocks at Burris. Somebody said something he couldn't make out, and the truck disappeared around a corner. He was astonished and disgusted. Suddenly his heart ached. And as if this humiliating affront to him had jostled the facts in his memory, he understood that this time wouldn't be any different from the half-dozen others when he'd set out to bind up the injuries of his love. Eileen wouldn't be home, or he would never get there, or, at the worst, it would turn out as it had the single time he'd actually confronted her: wearily she had called Critter to the door, and Burris had tried to get past him to explain himself to his wife. "Honey?" he'd kept saying. "Honey? I'm here, get your shit." At first Critter had done only the bare minimum necessary to restrain him, but it had all ended terribly, with Burris bloody-faced and hysterical and hand-cuffed to metal rings in the floor of a squad car. He hadn't even grasped that violence was being done—he was so intent on what he wanted to say to her—until he'd settled down at the police station, where blood dripped from his nose onto his bluejeans.

Standing now on Roosevelt Street while the evening steadily cooled off around him, he began to burn again with resentment. What had made him think he might ever forgive her? And how could she have done it to him, unless she felt only hatred of his very face? He turned this way and that on the sidewalk, com-pletely helpless to find the right direction. Motels, gas stations, and corner lamps swung through his sight. And how could she hate him now, when she had loved him then?

"You're like an alcoholic," Jeanine remarked. She was watching Burris shoot up.

Burris found it impossible to reply. The relentlessness of what he took to be Jeanine's stupidity always unnerved him.

"In your current material existence, what you're doing is, you're making all the wrong choices. We're here to make choices," she said. "You know what the Japanese say? First the man takes a drink. Then the drink takes a drink." She leaned forward. She was sitting on the divan. "Then the drink takes the man. Or maybe the Chinese, or somebody."

"If you make me spill this," Burris said, twisting together three paper matches, "I will beat you till I feel no anger." He struck the matches and, holding them in one hand as they burned, raised up the spoon with the other.

"Burris, let me talk to you just a few minutes before you—you know, before you get off."

"You wanna talk? Talk." Burris blew on the liquid in the spoon carefully to cool it.

"Talk is all I can do," Jeanine told him. "I can't do anything else." She reached to her big blue book beside her on the divan —and for an instant Burris sensed her, in the corner of his vision, as a poised and gracious white presence in the room, but kept the main of his attention on his spoon of liquefied heroin. Turning the pages of her book, Jeanine wrinkled her nose. "That stuff always smells like the inside of a cigaret when you get it cooked. Now. Lucifer, by rebelling against Christ Michael, became one of those who has succumbed to the urge of self and surrendered to spurious personal liberty."

"What the fuck?" Burris said. "Oh." He saw that she was reading.

"See? That's just where you're at, honey. Running up money in the wrong bank. You're opting for extinction every time you do up. You're kissing death"— and she began to read again: " 'Rejection of universe allegiance and disregard of fraternal obligations. Blindness to cosmic relationships.' Hey—I thought you were going to listen for a minute."

Burris pitied himself immensely even as he tapped the needle into the vein of his arm, because twenty dollars' worth was only a feeble joke, an almost pointless medicinal gesture, a parody of intoxication that might, nevertheless, help him sleep for a few hours. "I'm listening," he told Jeanine. "Fuck. Wish we had a fucking phone," he said absently.

"I'm just telling you what Lucifer was into. You know Lucifer? The Devil? But actually, the one we call the Devil is named Caligastia. He was a prince, it says, a deposed planetary prince of Urantia."

From his association with Jeanine, Burris understood that Urantia was the planet Earth. "You're so insane," he said, not without affection. As the heroin reached him, he could feel the sinuses at the back of his nose opening up.

Jeanine held the big *Urantia Book* in her lap, perusing it gaily like a family album. "The Lucifer Rebellion was a big flop. But it says, right here on page 609—listen: 'While Lucifer was deprived of all administrative authority in Satania, there then existed no local universe power nor tribunal which could detain or destroy this wicked rebel.' And then it says here that he's still operating, Burris—'Thus were these archrebels allowed to roam the entire system to seek further penetration for their doctrines of discontent and self-assertion.' It says here, 'They continue their deceptive and seductive efforts to confuse and mislead the minds of men and angels.' They're still operating a big business right here on Urantia."

"Well," Burris said, "I ain't exactly about to OD, but it works." He released a sigh as if he'd been holding his breath past any endurance. His sinuses were completely free. The gratitude of the survivor, the melting feminine gratitude of the saved, lit every follicle from within. "You look like an angel yourself, right now, you know that? In that white raincoat," he said. Suddenly nauseated by the taste of beer, he held out to her his half-finished Schlitz.

Angels

Jeanine came over and sat on the floor by the wicker chair, and took the beer and drank from it. He kissed her on top of her head, and she rested her head on his knee, putting her arms half about his waist. "I get contact vibes off you," she said to him. "When you get high, I get high." Peace settled down upon the midnight. Burris sat back into the silence and blindness of the heroin of Mexico: the silence that isn't empty and the blindness that isn't dark.

4

Jamie stood in the middle of the yard, apparently not
quite sure of the direction of the house, which was ten feet away,
or perhaps a little nonplussed, somewhat taken aback, possibly, by
the platter of fried chicken Bill Houston had just handed her. She
and Burris had been eating up those pills of his. It ran in the
family. Even Mrs. Houston herself, as she observed her son's
woman friend from the living room, was sipping from a large glass
of V-8 juice with vodka in it.

In the pitiless downpouring light of afternoon, Jamie's aura was
plainly visible to Mrs. Houston as an atmosphere of haze surrounding her, and Mrs. Houston caught her breath. Without the
tiniest avenue for escape, without the smallest meager hole
through which the nourishment of God might find her, Jamie was

hemmed in and completely owned by the Evil One. In this absolute bondage, Mrs. Houston saw clearly, her possible future daughter-in-law was permitted to live and move amid a trumped-up psychic ectoplasm of unconscious grace, because ultimately it was the black darkness of Satan that possessed her, and he bided his time. He was keeping Jamie for later. Jamie was going to be his dessert. Mrs. Houston began a prayer for her: only the ceaseless cries of those already saved might pierce the walls imprisoning this young woman who stood in the back yard obliterated on pills and red wine, looking ridiculous in her short cut-off jeans and purple high-heeled shoes, trying to decipher a tray of chicken.

William Junior manned the barbecue thing, and Burris was in the kitchen drumming his hands like a Congolese on the top of her radio while Jeanine concentrated on making a salad. Mrs. Houston cast her heart adrift amid a fluid affection, surrounded by all her sons. From her big chair in the living room, formerly Harold Carter Sandover's big chair, she could see her eldest making chicken, and hear her youngest in the kitchen—"Co-mo be-bee light my fi-yer," Burris was screaming—and see, out front, her middle son James, who had poked his torso under the hood of the green junked Ford out there. The baby was sleeping on Mrs. Houston's bed in the back of the house, and James's wife Stevie had her boy and Jamie's little girl in the bathroom, trying to get them cleaned up for supper. Mrs. Houston loved them all. It failed to disturb her, in this moment out of time, that some of these people had abandoned themselves to fate and become dangerous. It failed to trouble her just now that she had seen these pow-wows before among such men: in the midst of family gatherings they spoke casually and curtly just out of earshot. Terrible things happened later.

And suddenly out of nowhere, Jamie's little girl was standing there in front of her. It seemed she was about to say something. In the cool of the living room before the words came, distanced from the other voices and other sounds of the world, Mrs. Houston felt herself and the child enveloped in an utter loneliness, and she knew the others had forgotten all about them. "Can I take the hair off the corn?" the little girl asked her. Before Mrs. Houston could form any notion of what she was talking about, she was gone and might only have been a ghost.

Thy will be done, she said inside herself. And lately, in the last few years, she'd been able to mean it.

At the supper table, Jamie had sat on the floor instead of in her chair. "Hell of a thing," she was saying. "What the fuck here now," she said. "Whole place is greased, or something."

Stevie stood beside the table, waiting for folks to get arranged so that she could sit down. "You got a handful there, don't you?" she asked Bill Houston, who was helping Jamie up.

"Well, it's just temporary—you know, kind of an adjustment thing or whatever, I guess." His own eyes, drowned in gin, were like two setting suns.

Stevie said, "Just temporary means you can remember back when it was different. But it'll never be the same."

Everybody was crowded around the table in the kitchen now, except for the baby Ellen—and Burris, who, of all people, was in the back room feeding her some milk from her bottle. They ate the chicken and corn-on-the-cob off paper plates, and Wyatt spilled the sliced tomatoes of his salad into his lap. Burris came in after a while with the baby and sat jiggling her on his knee, making it hard for her to drink from the bottle he held to her mouth. "Look at them hands. Look at them fingers," he said. "They're just like for-real fingers, ain't they?" He ate nothing.

"Burris would make a great dad," Jeanine said. In the way of a reply there was a shocked silence. She said, "Well, he would. He's got this little model airplane that he made. He made it himself."

"I just wish Harry could be here to say grace," Mrs. Houston said. "But they got him up there with all the killers." She looked at no one, and appeared to be talking to her food.

"With all the *other* killers," Stevie said, irritated.

It was nearly six now, and the sun was turning the western rim of the sky to pink. Bill and James Houston stayed in the shadow of the old Ford's hood out front and watched while Burris moved off slowly down the street in James's pickup. "He won't be back," James remarked.

"He won't?"

"Not tonight. You give him any money?"

"I loaned him twenty dollars," Bill said. There was nothing further to add. It was one of those occasions for pretending your loved ones were without problems, and so one of those times when Burris could be expected to take swift advantage.

"Well, we ain't gonna fix this with these itty bitty pliers," James said. "And he's got all my tools."

"You fixing to tinker with this piece of shit? I mean seriously?"

James laughed and threw the pliers up and caught them one time. "I just hate to be in amongst all that mayhem in there." He gestured at the house. Over the little distance between it and them, no sound carried. Softened under the later light, its color-lessness was starting to appear subtle rather than drab, and some-thing about the quality of its peace would have given the passerby to know that a family was gathered within. Inside, Baby Ellen slept. The other two children sat by themselves on the living room floor, looking at an enormous picture-book Bible, while Wyatt described the story of David and Goliath for Miranda. Nobody had yet turned on any lights, though it was beginning to grow dark. In the kitchen the two younger women sat with Mrs. Hous-ton. Jamie was balanced in her chair, looking something like a huge Raggedy Ann, staring out of the jungle of hammers and white blindness in her mind. Stevie drank a cup of coffee and nodded rhythmically at her mother-in-law's talk: "I'll be seventy come August, God willing." Stevie knew Mrs. Houston would be seventy next August. It was Stevie's policy to cut her off before she got started, to remind her that everybody had heard it all before, but tonight Stevie felt stayed by the lethargy of familial sentiment, to be here with her husband's mother in a darkening house, and she was content to let her mother-in-law persist in her delusion that she was entertaining Jamie, as if Jamie were capable of feeling entertained.

"I was thirty-three years old before I ever bore a child," Mrs. Houston was saying. "I cried out in my heart to the Lord that I was a waste of a woman, married twelve years—and the Reverend John Miller laid his hand across my forehead on my birthday of 1945—in a holy church, I'm ashamed to tell you, that has since been turned into some kind or other of a skating roller-rink. And one week after that laying on of hands, they dropped the biggest bomb ever on the Japanese." She picked up a piece of celery and then, as if startled by the feel of it, let it drop. "And on that day when they told about the bomb on Japan, I knew without ever asking no doctor that I was growing a boy inside of me." She was talking to her home, and not to either of these women, from whom she felt estranged and by whom she felt mildly despised.

In the yard, the two men talked of the future. "Man named Dwight Snow," James was saying, "you ever hear of him? Dude's a maestro."

"A maestro? I never heard of him. Was he in Florence?"

"Nope." James tossed his empty beer can into the car through its rear window. "He was not in Florence."

"Well, I don't know if I want to work with somebody who don't know the same people I know. Who does he know? Where was he away?"

"He don't know anybody. He wasn't away anywhere."

Bill Houston put his hands in the pockets of his jeans and started walking in a tight circle. "I don't get it, James," he said.

"This guy is clean! No record, no unsavory associates, no nothing."

"And you want to walk in some place with him and do bad stuff? I don't get it."

"Don't you get it?" James was annoyed with his brother now, and kicked the side of the car and shook his head. "He just ain't been *caught,* man, because he's *good.*"

"That's what he says, huh? That what he tells you, James?"

"Hey—he's got at least two hundred thousand dollars' worth of diamonds, which he is currently in the process of fencing."

"You seen them?"

"I seen them. And at least he knows fences. He ain't a choirboy."

"It's just—well," Bill Houston said. "I just don't know."

"This person is a scholar of armed robbery, is what I'm saying. He *reads* about all this shit. He's done it, and he's talked to the people who've done it, and I'm telling you he knows, all, about it." James leaned back against the Ford. "Hey, you ought to see them diamonds. Little rainbows, man. You hold them in your hand, feels like you're getting your dick sucked." He looked carefully at his brother's face. "I thought you were looking for some shit to get into, Bill Junior."

"Well, I am."

"Well, I'm vouching for this man and I'm vouching for this situation. If it sounds like there's a few hazards in it, then welcome to the West, Big Bro."

Bill Houston looked off into the shimmering distance, in which a DC-10, the slow lumbering picture of world-weariness, was taking off into the sky. "It's still hot," he said.

"You wanna make some money, Bill Junior? Because I am. And so is Burris."

"Burris?"

"Burris is all grown up now."

"Burris?" Bill Houston felt the day's last heat getting to him. Though his perspiration dried on leaving his pores, he knew he was sweating because his eyes burned with its salt. He shook his head, but it only made him feel dizzier. "Burris can't really handle something like this, can he?"

"He's all grown up now, Bill Junior. If I got to work partners, I'd like to keep it in the family as much as I can."

"Well well," Bill Houston said. "Hm."

"You want to make some money?" His brother clasped his arm. "Money right or wrong?"

Bill Houston had always liked the sound of it. "Yeah," he said. "Money right or wrong."

They both looked over in the direction of the house. Although they'd never been comrades in youth, separated as they were by several years, there was something like the guilt of childhood conspiracies in the way they stood together. "Mom's different," James said suddenly. "I don't like the way she talks. She talks like there's nobody there listening."

"I know what you mean."

"You know what I'm saying? I wish she'd quit."

"Why don't you tell her?" Bill Houston said.

"I want to tell her, but then all of a sudden I just don't. Very weird."

"I don't get it," Bill Houston said. "Why don't you just walk up and tell her she looks the wrong direction when she talks?"

"Well, why don't you?"

"Because—I don't know," Bill Houston said. His stomach felt tight, and he wished he hadn't eaten so much. "It's hard to explain that shit to your own mother," he said.

Dwight Snow and James and Bill Houston sat in frayed lounge chairs out back, shaded by a green corrugated plastic awning of which James was quite proud. They drank coffee, looking off the patio into the back yard like people waiting for a show of entertainment to start. But it was just a lawn of overgrown brown weeds, and up against the fence, beside the back gate, a stack of assorted scraps of decomposing lumber.

Before long, Dwight commanded the drift of talk. What had begun as a general description of their plans for the Central Avenue First State Bank turned into a display of his knowledge. "I picked up that pistol when I was twenty-one," he said. "In six years I have never heard a siren, never heard an alarm go off, never seen an officer of the law on my tail. I have been, and intend to remain, one hundred percent successful as a bandit." His eyes did not once flicker from Bill Houston's face.

"You do any B-and-E's?" Bill Houston asked. The morning was getting hot and the coffee was making his stomach ache and he was irritated all out of proportion by Dwight Snow. But he wondered how Dwight had come by his diamonds.

"Burglary is insanity," Dwight said. "I should know, I've done enough of it. You walk around on tiptoe and you have absolutely no control over your environment, no idea what's waiting for you in there. You could walk your face right up some vigilante's twelve-gauge. Some psycho who's been sitting by his bed fully loaded and paranoid every night of his life. I feel much more comfortable doing business in the daytime with my neighborhood savings and loan association, or my local jeweler's. I know who has the firepower—*me*—and I know exactly who's there, where they're located, and what they're doing, before I ever make a move. The environment is one hundred percent mine—or I go home. I can always come back tomorrow, right? I can just say 'pass' on any situation where I'm not sure of outmaneuvering the opposing forces.

"Now, a bank—okay, you've never done a bank, either of you. Fine. You're in for a pleasant surprise. Ten seconds after you're in session, it no longer feels like a robbery. It feels more like your average daily simple transaction. Because these people are trained to cash checks, and they're trained to make loans and various transactions—traveller's checks, etcetera—and, these people are trained to be robbed. They're *briefed* on that, see—it's no fucking skin off their ass if they give you the best of service here, the money's all insured—they *want* it to go smooth. They're instructed to put up no resistance, obey orders, and minimize risk all around. I tell them I don't want to take home any funny money, I don't want to hear any alarms or have to deal with any police—I demand and I expect full cooperation from all employees present. And I *get* it. I go to pick up a stack of bills, they say, 'Uh-uh, excuse me, sir, that's wired to trip an alarm, excuse me, sir, these bills are marked, that drawer trips a silent call'— I mean to tell you, gentlemen. In this venture profit outweighs risk a hundred to one or better."

With this last statement he settled back lightly in his chair and removed his hat, a red baseball cap of plastic mesh bearing a patch on the front. What irritated Bill Houston about him was the efficiency of his gestures and the precision of his speech: in his own mind Houston linked these qualities with homosexuals, schoolteachers, and chicken military officers. Dwight took off his glasses—Bill Houston noticed that he lacked an index finger— and his eyes were revealed to be enormous, as blue as the sea and as liquid, with long lashes like a woman's or a child's, yet hooded by their lids like a reptile's. He seemed lost in his vision of illegal transactions now, wiping his face carefully with a folded white hankie. Houston noticed that his red cap was lined with what appeared to be tin foil, shining in the morning sun.

When they were done talking it was nearly noon. Dwight left by the back gate, the way he'd arrived.

Bill and James lingered on the patio, stupefied by a mounting humidity and mesmerized by the doings of a gargantuan truck in the alley behind James's home. Bill Houston couldn't shake a sense of identification with its hunger as it closed with, uplifted, and showered itself with the contents of a green rubbish dumpster. A rapid changing in the timbre of the atmosphere, as clouds formed out of nothing overhead and oppressed the light, gave to these few moments the unreal quality of an animated cartoon. As the big truck moved down the alley, stopping every hundred feet or so to devour more stinking debris, lightning passed from cloud to land at the horizon, and great drops of water started falling all around them. The smell of it on the asphalt streets left them breathless. "I never mind this kind of a storm," James said. Its clatter on the awning over their heads was deafening. "It's gonna flood," James announced, "and I'm gonna get drunk real slow."

The brothers came in from the patio to get a couple of beers. James liked to mix his with lemonade. "Hey, you oughta do something or other for her," he said when they encountered Jamie, who was relaxing furiously before the television in a canvas chair. Wearing a teeshirt and cut-offs, her legs crossed Indian-style, she zeroed her gaze microscopically at *The Wild World of Animals* and sucked on a glass of ice-and-wine in the hope of drawing herself back from what she considered to be the edge of things.

"I figure, just leave her alone till whatever it is goes through its whole life-span," Bill Houston said. "I can't afford to get involved. Her kind of trouble, the kind she's deep into right this minute— it has a million little doodads in it. Like the insides of a watch, do you know what I mean, James?" They fell silent, watching the show's host frolic with some leopard cubs outside of his safari tent. It bothered Bill Houston that Jamie was turning into the kind of person you could talk about when she was right there in the room with you.

He sat on the couch which, by night, was Miranda's bed. Before him stretched a day without prospect, but he experienced no boredom. He had stepped onto the nearest moving thing. They'd made their plans. They were going to do a job. Count-down. Even the ordinary things were invested with life, and he looked forward with interest to the next television show. "Bas-tard's kinda wiry for an old guy," Jamie said, meaning the gentle-man on the screen. She chewed the ice from her drink energetically, banging the empty glass on the instep of her foot over and over.

James brought two beers downstairs from the kitchen and sat beside his brother on the couch. A midday news-break came on the television, talking about the Dow Jones, making mention of some unimportant activities of the President. "What the fuck *is* the Dow Jones, anyways?" Jamie said. "Man!" she shouted sud-denly, stretching her bare legs out before her as if electrified. "I'm just faking a feeling," she said.

James changed the channel. "What feeling is that?"

"I just entirely cannot use any of this shit. Intensely. I mean other days have seen me reeling and rocking and rolling, but right now I don't even know the name of that town."

James said, "What town is that?"

"The Town of Love. Or whatever the fuck. You know."

"Boy," James said. "Your reels are really spinning."

"I got a handle on what I'm saying, even if you don't," she said.

She got up and walked, balancing at first as if trying to stand up in a rowboat, to the stairs and then up the stairs to the kitchen.

Bill and James watched the start of the local *Dialing for Dollars*. "You have to be on a list for this thing?" James wondered. "Seven hunnerd and eighty-seven dollars. I hope they call us." His voice seemed to wash away on the damp noise of the rain.

Jamie returned with another drink. Stevie was out cruising second-hand stores with a cousin, and the two five-year-olds were at the TinyTown Daycare. Baby Ellen was playing with a mobile stretched above her head across the bassinet, her fascination continually renewed for things that were always the same. For the moment, commonalities of blood and time and place made them very much a family, as the rain came down in sheets onto the patio, filling the air with the musty odor of ammonia and wetting down a city that had seen no moisture in weeks.

Nobody was watching the show. James brought a pitcher of lemonade and a fifth of Gordon's Gin down from the kitchen. He chased straight gin with a mixture of beer and lemonade. Bill Houston sat still, enjoying and enduring the tick of his heart through a day of rain. Countdown. He kicked off his boots. "I mean," he said, "I want to do some business—take a chance, make some money—and this guy is talking like we're going to engage the enemy, James. 'Outmaneuver the opposing forces.' He can outmaneuver my dick when it goes up his rectum."

James shrugged. "Only game in town."

"How'd he get that finger took off? He ever say?"

"Snake bit it, I think," James said.

"Well, I don't know. I think he's just one of these rabid evil Nazi worshipers. There's no place for him with the regular folks of the world. He's heading straight for the joint whether he knows it or not, and when he gets there they're going to give him a hat and make him a secret colonel in the Aryan Brotherhood."

James laughed. "He already got him a real nice hat."

"Yeah—what's it say on it again? 'Alterna?' "

"Alterna," James said.

"What's that? Alterna."

"He tells me it's a kind of snake."

"And he keeps tin foil inside of it. What's that supposed to be for?"

James was beginning to look a little nervous. "Well, he says it keeps out the E-rays."

"E-rays. Did you say E-rays?"

"Yes I did."

"There really any such thing as E-rays?"

"I wouldn't know about that, Bill Junior. There ain't any tin foil in my hat, is all I know."

"This is our leader," Bill Houston said. "A young dude with tin foil on his head."

"What can I say?" James said. "Your complaint is noted."

Ellen began to fuss and whine in the bassinet, gaining seriousness with every breath, mounting toward wails of outrage. "Calling Mom," Jamie said. "Baby to Mom. Come in, Mom. Calling Mom." The rain fell. The TV talked. One breath after another. Countdown.

She was drinking a beer in Dwight Snow's car in the Bashas' parking lot, a shimmering lake of molten asphalt, and training the air conditioner's vents onto her face. Though she'd pushed it up to MAX, the unit was feeble against the heat; when it blew in her face, her knees felt hot; the back seat area was twenty degrees warmer than the front. Dwight was now in the supermarket buying lemons and tequila. He had a pretty nice car here, a Buick Riviera with a red interior that still smelled new. She didn't know how she got into these places.

Holding the can of beer between her knees, she took an amphetamine capsule from an envelope in her shirt pocket—a Black Beauty, courtesy of the youngest of the Houston brothers—and chewed it slowly. She'd gotten so she liked to break them up with her teeth, liked the bitter taste, the black taste—it *was* black beauty, wasn't it? All I eat anymore.

The rear-view mirror returned her face to her, cavern-cheeked and bug-eyed, and when she drew her lips apart she looked into the image of canine hysteria, the teeth yielding a purple tint from days on end of red wine. Almost like a physical reality, somewhere in the upper left quadrant of her chest there lurked true knowledge of what she was doing; and in the remaining three-quarters of her psyche the word on chemical abuse was Fuck You. A person needs pills for the world and wine for the pills. Anything further I'll let you know.

It was kicking in now: the day looked brighter, and the random slow-jerk of vehicles and figures in the parking lot around her took on the satisfying rhythms and choreography of a dance. The radio's hillbilly voices prayed for terror—

> *On the thirty-first floor*
> *A gold-plated door*
> *Won't keep out the Lord's burning rain—*

and a cream-colored Lincoln, driven by a Mexican youth wearing a monstrous white cowboy hat, drove very very slowly through the field of her vision. Suddenly she thought of how the light off the snow in Chicago turned the white buildings pink in the later afternoon. With a trembling hand she turned off the radio. She looked down at her rubber-thonged feet, wiggling her toes with their golden nails. Since coming to Phoenix, she'd discovered she greatly relished painting her toenails and fingernails, enjoyed removing the polish and painting them again, sometimes spending a few hours at it, drinking a little red table wine and decorating her extremities—she was startled by the opening of the car's door and a rush of hot wind. Dwight seated himself behind the wheel, tossing the sack of margarita fixings into the back seat. "Magic carpet," he said. He turned on the radio and tuned in a classical station and put it all in motion.

They were in the suburbs east of the city hardly long enough for her to appreciate the fact; and then the immaculate serenity of high-rent developments gave out, and Jamie and Dwight confronted flat fields—gone winter cotton, and rows lying fallow—that moved away from them as if shot from something enormous toward low hills, and beyond the hills toward distant mountains dissolving into clouds, dark, hallucinatory, and vague. Dwight drove into this emptiness and stopped the car.

"Ain't there no more town?" she asked.

"You know what that is over there?" Dwight said, pointing to a conglomerate of modernesque buildings set down in the midst of these vast fields. "That's a college. A community college. For college boys and college girls." He leaned forward and tapped his knuckles against the front windshield of his Riviera as if this action might dislodge the images of human structures from the glass. "Their school mascot, their symbol—the symbol of all their education—is the artichoke. I'm not pulling your leg, Jamie. Their team is called the Artichokes. The school colors are pink and green. To them it's all a joke. And they own all this land." He pointed behind them with his stub of an index finger, sweeping it through three hundred sixty degrees around the car. "Rich people have too much money. I intend to do something about that."

"I heard your finger got eaten by a snake," Jamie remarked.

"I was bitten by a rattlesnake," he said. "I'm allergic to the anti-venom, so I lost the finger."

She watched his profile—one giant blue eye behind the kind of glasses Clark Kent wore; one nearly jaw-length sideburn; half a mustache that was growing into a handlebar. Beneath his baseball cap he wore his hair fairly short. He looked like a person who might know how to get away with things but who really didn't care whether he got away with them or not. His gaze was practiced and direct: he looked exactly like a convict. Alarms began going off in the fields around them. "Did Bill tell you I got raped over in Chicago?"

He moved his attention from the fields to her face. "Somebody said something about it."

She wanted to be clear: "If you touch me you will die."

He blinked twice. The classical music played—some kind of piano—and the nozzle of the air conditioner spewed cool air. "I'll drink to that," he said, and reached for the shopping bag in the back seat. "You'll find a knife in the glove compartment," he told her, peering into the sack and selecting a lemon.

From under various maps protruded the black handle of a switchblade. Opening it she startled herself—it almost flew from her fingers when she touched the button. Dwight placed a lemon on the dash before her. "Get us a couple thin slices, okay?" Taking the bottle of Jose Cuervo Gold from the sack, he removed its cap and savored its aroma.

Jamie hacked at the lemon, holding it awkwardly in midair. To the right of the car something moved, and then it wasn't there. Blood flowed from her thumb. "Starting to see things out of the corner of my eye. Over my shoulder, kind of like."

Dwight tore a strip of paper from the shopping bag, and she wrapped it around her thumb and finished slicing.

But now Dwight seemed to have forgotten the tequila. "I wrote

several screenplays in the Army, which I would like to see produced. Prospects would be considerably enhanced if I could see
to the financing myself. One was a sequel for the Smokey and the
Bandit films—*Smokey and the Bandit III.* The return on invest-
ment there could be very impressive. That's why we've kind of
entered into this arrangement, me and the three Houston brothers. One of whom you are connected with intimately."

"If you're trying to tell me you guys got some excitement lined
up for yourselves, forget it. I know all about it." But why hadn't
anyone told her exactly what was happening? Hot wires of rage
flared in her skull, and it was all she could do to keep them from
breaking out of her temples. They'd all been keeping her in the
dark, like a child in a house of sickness.

"I just want you to know we're not all fucked-up cowboys here.
In this business I usually find myself working with individuals who
can't see past getting a little cash in hand. But I see this project
as one piece, one step along the way. One assesses one's talents
and does whatever is necessary to, like, maximize their potential.
Make them bear fruit."

"One gets one's jive down and starts talking one's shit." She
ate another capsule out of her shirt.

"I can be a real force in the film industry," Dwight insisted.

The clouds were wild and black and slowly moving. It was the
flattest field she had ever seen. Dwight rested his arm on the seat,
around back of her, the fingers light on her shoulder. "We're all
in this general project, all of us together," he said. His arm was
definitely around her. She thought it infinitely strange. "But some
of us are doing one thing, and others are into something else
entirely. It's like this," he said, and turned his huge eyes upon her.
"There are some people who are in business, who move in the
realm of profit and loss pure and simple"—his mouth appeared
to her suddenly as a flapping vagina, a woman's sex—"and who
just naturally pick up that pistol when trying to locate capital.

Then there are these low-IQ trigger-pullers who just like to play very very rough, especially with themselves. They think dying by the gun is noisy enough that it must make sense and they figure it just can't hurt that much, something that noisy." Something was happening to the bottoms of the clouds—as the sun lowered into the space beneath them and touched the mountains, they burned with a pure golden light. "Some are in it for profit, Jamie, and others are in it for loss." Those eyes were eating her face. "Just be aware," he said, "that duplicates are being eliminated."

On most levels she didn't follow at all; and then on another level she understood perfectly, the level where methedrine married itself to every word. Rather unexpectedly it occurred to her that her husband Curt, about whom she scarcely ever thought, had been a nice person. These people were not. She knew that she was in a lot of trouble: that whatever she did would be wrong. The darkness—the nothing—the absent places behind doors and inside of things—she looked out at fields in the grip of a miraculous sundown. "You are one scary person," she told Dwight Snow. "I won't be surprised when they put a stop to you."

He took a lemon slice from her lap, unwrapped her finger of its brown bandage, squeezed a red drop onto the pale yellow moon as he held it. "You heard of blood rituals? Cannibal rites?"

"Don't."

"This is that. That's where we are." He chased tequila by biting the bloody fruit.

And then they were passing again over the abrupt verge between cotton fields and suburbs, zigzagging generally south and west so that the freshly opened model homes of townhouse developments soon gave up chasing them, and they shot into the terrain of gas stations, barbecue joints, and vacant lots full of trash, the territory of mutilated billboards and stucco walls of black graffiti, of low deteriorating buildings and trailers airing the handmade signboards of casual enterprise: AMMO FOR LESS; IN

THE NAME OF JESUS GUARANTEE USED TIRES; BROADWAY BARBER SHOP; PALM READER; SOUTHSIDE DRIVE-THRU TUNE-UP $$20$$. When they returned to James's house, she stuck her head around the side of the staircase to see who was downstairs. James was sitting alone in the living room, in the canvas chair, staring out through the sliding glass doors into the back yard. Becoming aware of her, he raised up two fingers in a sign of peace. She followed Dwight up into the kitchen.

"How do you know fences?" Bill Houston asked.

Dwight was looking at Jamie. She didn't look at him, but continued quartering lemons and limes. "For a couple years I made my living breaking into places and taking things," Dwight said. "Slice them thinner," he said to her. "I don't want to drink the lemon, I just want to taste it. So I made the acquaintance of a fence by the simple expedient of contacting an individual who'd just been fucking busted for B-and-E." He took off his Clark Kent glasses and rubbed his eyes and looked at Bill Houston. "His names was in the papers."

"And he gave you his fence?" Bill asked.

"I didn't go as somebody who needed from him. I appeared as somebody he should be afraid of. And I appeared to his fence as someone his fence should be afraid of. And today I have a very good fence. Toast with me," he said to Jamie, pouring out shots of tequila into two coffee mugs. He held the salt shaker above his upturned face, spilling some of its contents into his mouth—crystalline sparks, each separately visible through Jamie's amphetamine fast-shutter—and handed the shaker to her.

Looking at Bill Houston, she shook salt into her mouth, too. Dwight took her hand, linked his arm around hers at the elbow, and put a mug into her grasp. "To crime." Down the hatch. Each took a bite of lemon.

Jamie handed Bill Houston the salt shaker and performed the identical ritual with him, her elbow locked with his, each holding a mug of tequila. She hooked her leg around his at the knee. She stared into his face. "Don't shut me out of this," she said.

"Who's shutting you out?" he said. "You're standing right here. I don't give a shit."

"Okay," she said.

"I mean"—he looked at Dwight curiously—"why don't we just put it in a window somewheres?"

Dwight poured out three more. "I thought she was family."

"I am," Jamie said. "If I ain't, then it comes as a surprise to me, because I been travelling everywhere with this man."

"Travelling?" Dwight said. "Neat."

They all three kicked back another shot. The silence went on long enough that it got to be a thing. "Nobody trusts anybody in this kitchen," Jamie said. She left their presence, walking swiftly down the stairs and through the living room.

She stepped out into the yard carrying half a lemon. In the bare patches around her the dirt boiled. She was sufficiently aware of the temperature to have been able to mention it, but she did not *feel heat.*

It's kill or be killed.

Digging her thumbnail into the pulp, she felt the juice of lemon cells explode against her palm. *They're coming for you.* The skin rippled on her back. Something had touched her back. *Do it.*

Do what? They were confusing her. They were deep and ragged and vivid, two or three of them talking all at once.

She went back inside. The TV was on, and it said, *The President's order has been disobeyed. Only ten more days.*

.   .   .

Bill Houston woke up. It was the middle of the night. He felt strange and unprepared.

It took him a minute to understand that he was in his brother's house, that Baby Ellen had been crying and had awakened him. Jamie was up with her, across the living room, and the light was on. Evidently she'd just carried the baby back down from the kitchen, where they'd been warming up a bottle of milk. She sat down, holding Ellen in the crook of her arm, and for a heartbeat, while she reached with her other hand to switch on the radio, she held the baby's bottle between her shoulder and chin the way she might have done with a telephone receiver, keeping the rubber nipple in the baby's mouth. She kept the volume on the radio very low, and the music faded in and out, an old Four Tops tune which Bill Houston recognized from another time and another place. He propped himself on an elbow, spying on her, it felt like, because she was unaware of him now. She wore a teeshirt and otherwise nothing. A purple bruise covered the instep of her left foot. I know half a dozen people your age who are dead already, he wanted to tell her.

Baby Ellen was asleep now. With gentle care, Jamie put her back into her bassinet, and checked on Miranda, who slept, covered by a leather jacket, on the sofa. The announcer identified the station and the hour—Little Rock, where it was four in the morning—and then his voice receded as the signal washed away in the weather of distant mountains, and Bill Houston had one of those vivid experiences of being adrift, a revelation of how completely helpless they were, the only ones awake in a great darkness, the only light anywhere—God was about to speak— God was here—they were in God's mouth, this light—and he watched in wonder and dread as Jamie unscrewed the nipple and tipped the bottle of translucent blue plastic to her lips and drank the milk.

The three brothers picked Dwight up at the corner of Broadway and Central at nine in the morning. He was standing in front of a fried chicken establishment holding a brown paper shopping sack filled with various items for disguise, his foot resting on an olive-drab duffel bag containing two revolvers, a German machine pistol, and a sawed-off twenty-gauge shotgun with a shortened stock. "Friends and neighbors," Dwight said. Anything could go wrong now.

The four-door mid-size Chrysler the men travelled in was not quite stolen. It had been marked for repossession by one of Dwight Snow's rivals, and the Houstons had repossessed it first. Burris started to get out from behind the wheel, but Dwight stayed him with a hand. "Just let me have the keys. From this point forward, you don't ever leave that driver's seat till we're through with this car."

"No keys," Burris said. "We busted open the trunk and wired it shut."

"Good. No problem." Dwight put the duffel bag into the trunk.

He sat in the back seat next to Bill Houston and dealt out things from his shopping bag—a mustache for James, big round sunglasses for Bill, for Burris a ridiculous grey beard. "Nobody's going to look too close at a person in a car," Dwight explained to Burris, "so it doesn't matter how phony you look. We just want facial camouflage all around. Flowers?"

James, in the front seat, reached down by his feet and handed over a bouquet of wildflowers wrapped in green paper, a gift item sold on the street corners of the city by half-dressed young women. "Here, darling."

Dwight took the flowers and removed a few. "Hey, why don't we put these in our buttonholes? A little class. Just for appearances' sake." His neat efficiency, as he gripped each flower by its stem between thumb and forefinger; as he looked into the face of each man, handing him a flower; as he moved his eyes in a continual round of the scene outside the vehicle—rear street, Mexican joint, intersection, Kentucky fried, street forward—was inspiring to the others. Bill Houston, sitting beside him, observing his partners, feeling the sun begin to warm the Chrysler's interior, felt a narrowing and focusing of his own dry-mouthed fear.

"Where we gonna stop and break out weapons?" James asked.

"Wow. I have to pee. I have to piss so bad," Burris said. Bill Houston didn't like to hear the undercurrent of whining in his youngest brother's tone of voice. It turned his stomach. It made him afraid.

Dwight leaned forward and put a hand on Burris's shoulder. "You are the weakest link in this operation. We're taking you right up to your limit. But you're with us because I am absolutely certain that you'll smoothly and efficiently carry out everything required of you today. Understand?"

"Sure," Burris said.

"You know your job. You stay parked out front as long as it takes. What if we never come out?"

"I never move."

"A-plus. You never move. You stay there as long as it takes. You're going to feel anxious, but you're not going to move. If I thought you were the kind to break, somebody else would be driving this car. Now we'll stop at a gas station and bring the guns up front, and you can piss. Head over to Seventh Street."

It was as if the hand on Burris's shoulder communicated serenity. He relaxed.

Under Dwight Snow's direction he drove slowly over to Seventh Street and then north to a gas station of dubious quality, keeping his right hand at all times on the dashboard and its thumb on the buttons of the radio, pushing the buttons regularly to change the stations and cut off the DJ's and get the talking out of his life.

When Burris was finished in the bathroom he came back and rested against the car while Bill Houston went inside to empty his bladder. Bill Houston didn't like the way Burris looked. Anything could go wrong now. He could step outside to find squad cars flanking the Chrysler, thanks to the merest bit of the vast unforeseen, the unconsiderable factors and the twists of dumb luck.

In the hacked and vandalized service station restroom he stood before the commode with one hand on his hip, unzipping the fly of his pants—but when he saw the tiny specks of blood dotting the mirror's glass above the sink, he lost any desire to relieve himself and his stomach turned hard as ice. He felt he was looking, now, at what hadn't been foreseen.

"What do you think you're trying to do?" he said to Burris when he stepped outside. "You figure we're just playing here? You think we're going to get high and then go to the drive-in?"

Dwight was at that moment getting out of the car and going around to the trunk. "Problem, Bill?" He untied the wire, raised the trunk's lid, and hoisted out the duffel bag full of firearms.

"This son of a bitch went in there and shot his arm full of dope," Bill Houston said. "There's blood on the mirror in there."

"Blood on the mirror," Dwight repeated.

"I used to play cards with a couple dopers on the Reservation up by Tacoma," Bill Houston told his brother. "They were always spraying shit on the wall like that when they were done shooting up. You think I don't know what that blood is?" He appealed to Dwight: "Didn't even try to hide it," he said.

Burris shrugged, examining his boots and behaving as if there were something on one of his boots that needed to be scraped away.

"I ought to jerk your fucking head off for you," Bill Houston said. He was on the brink of tears.

"We'll discuss this in a minute. I've got to get these out of the public eye," Dwight said, and moved to carry the duffel bag into the bathroom. "Bring the flowers," he told James over his shoulder. "Burris, stay with the car."

When Bill and James had joined him inside, James holding the bouquet of flowers, Dwight said, "I think we should just proceed as planned." He knelt on the floor and took the machine pistol from the duffel bag along with two boxes of rounds. "If he's too high to function, we can improvise."

James had nothing to say. He looked deep into the mirror stained with grease and a string of minute bloody flecks; his expression, as he greeted his own face, like that of someone suddenly released.

"Improvise?" Bill Houston said. "Jesus Christ, improvise?" He accepted the sawed-off shotgun from Dwight, and then a box of one dozen shells. He looked about them at the walls and floor of the obliterated john, but couldn't find anything to point to that would explain why he felt it necessary to abort their plans. "Hey," he said to James finally. "Unwrap them daisies, how about." He broke open his weapon and began inserting shells. It was a pump-action Remington, and it made him feel happy in spite of himself.

"You never can tell. He just might function with a little more finesse." Dwight opened his garish tropical shirt and slipped the machine pistol into a holster rigged with a cowboy belt and black electrician's tape that girded his chest, the pistol resting along his rib cage under his left arm. He helped Bill Houston unwrap and re-wrap the flowers, the sawed-off Remington now among them. James loaded both revolvers—a nine-millimeter Ruger of stainless steel and his own long-barrelled Colt—and replaced them in the duffel bag along with the boxes of ammunition.

They all three stood up straight and looked at one another—Bill Houston clutching the lethal bouquet, James with the duffel bag, Dwight holding his arm close alongside like the victim of a stroke—with something akin to love, a kind of immense approval, because now they were in one another's hands.

"I'm getting excellent vibes here," Dwight said. "Obviously no one wants to scrap this thing. Let's just take it along the projected route. If Burris fucks up, we'll shut down and do it all over again tomorrow."

Neither brother dissented. The time was now, it was obvious.

Burris had another shrug for them when the three got into the car and nobody said anything except, "Drive on." He knew they sensed his incompetence. "Where's my piece?" he said.

"In the bag here. You can keep my little monster when we go into it," James told him. "I'm taking the Ruger." As he said these things he looked out of the window, and spoke casually.

Burris followed Dwight's orders carefully, turning west only when directed, north only when directed, taking it one block at a time. He wanted them to know that he was competent: that half a bag—not a lethal dose, by any means—was just about right here, focusing his attention and rounding off some of the corners. He was in a good place, and felt relief beyond the mere action of heroin: he'd taken a chance getting off like this, that went without saying. He could have taken too much, he understood that. But sometimes the proper induction of chemicals was a requirement. He was surprised when Dwight said, "Stop here." They were in front of the Central Avenue First State Bank. "We've come to where the flavor is," James said. He set the forty-four Colt on the seat between them, touching Burris's thigh. "Street looks sunny and calm," Bill Houston said, and Dwight said, "Remember: motor running at all times."

And Burris's Adam's apple filled with wet cement and his eyes clouded with burning teardrops. "We're going to be seven minutes maximum," he heard Dwight's voice telling him. "But suppose we're in there for seven hours?"

"Nothing," Burris said. "I stay here," he said. Although he knew they all knew he wasn't competent.

They went into it slowly, testing each inch of space.

As they went into it James felt his nostrils dilate painfully, and jism dripped from his penis and stained his underwear. The stainless steel barrel of the revolver touched his thigh like a loving finger, and he said to it in his mind, You're everything to me. For the next seven minutes you are my wife, my lawyer, and my money.

Shallow breath now, he told himself, and drew oxygen slowly. The odor of wildflowers, as beside him his brother shifted his bouquet from one hand to the other, was overpowering. The bank opened away from his face like a tremendous bell to be kept absolutely silent. Every surface was capable of ringing.

James had walked past these windows many times in recent weeks, on the other side of the glass, and had thought himself familiarized. But he hadn't been prepared, somehow, for the largeness of it all, for the insignificance of the people surrounding them, as if this great chamber with its oversized plants and tall, thin fountain of water had been constructed for a race of monsters. He wanted to detain his partners, invite them to get a sense of the place. But it was too late. It was already in progress. Bill Houston went past the high semicircular security desk, the elderly guard elevated by some means—perhaps on a platform—without looking at the man. James was happy with the calm manner in which his brother laid out his flowers on one of the check-writing counters and folded his hands over the package, staring forward at the row of tellers' windows. Dwight moved to the officers' area in the rear and, his back to the several desks where a few men and women pored over figures or chatted with customers seeking favors, he put his left hand to the buttons of his Hawaiian print shirt.

James went deliberately to the guard's C-shaped desk and leaned against it, putting his right hand at belt-level beneath the hem of his shirt, fingers brushing the Ruger's grip. The guard, immaculate, silver-haired, and gentlemanly, looked down at James through pale grey eyes, and it seemed to James that they looked straight into each other's minds, that both of them understood completely the requirements and parameters of this situation. He'd been about to speak inconsequentially—this the bank that gives toasters? don't I know you from Thursday bowling?— and chat till the signal came down. But now he saw the understanding in this person's eyes and froze completely: *he knows.* He knows; he's going to draw out on me; goddamn it, Dwight, let me see the nod or I'll start this thing myself—

Dwight nodded once. The weapons came out.

Dwight called out clearly, "Ladies and gentlemen: your money is my money."

James put the Ruger up against the guard's nose. Bill Houston raised the shotgun high to advertise his power and cried, "We want everything completely quiet!"—although no one had said a word or made a noise of any kind. The single audible sound was the action of water on water as the oblivious fountain ceaselessly fell into its pool—a sound all mixed up with the crashing of blood in James's arteries, his pulse so urgent he could feel it in the palm of his hand where he gripped the revolver. Most of those present —there were no more than a dozen customers this morning, some in the tellers' line, a couple at the counters, two or three at the desks with the bank's officers—found some reason to look away, not yet understanding that they represented hazard to these bandits and would be required to move. One man went on writing in his checkbook next to the torn green wrappings of the bouquet, a multi-hued assortment of wildflowers scattered at his feet, his head lowered—ignoring the armed man who stood with feet braced apart not two yards from his elbow—refusing any connection with this mysterious and violent event.

They were in it.

In the rear, Dwight was briefly manhandling the chiefest officer available, speaking too softly for James to hear. Bill Houston covered the tellers and intervening customers. James pressed the Ruger into the guard's face, making him smell the stainless steel: as soon as the money came out he would have to come around and disarm the man, and then take tellers one and two. Between James and Bill were customers who could not be said to be thoroughly neutralized. They were thin—they had known they'd be thin—but it meant as much as ten thousand dollars each to take the bank without a fourth gun.

Dwight was speaking now: "All right, we're in Phase Two, control and movement." To the tellers: "I want *no alarms.*" To the officers: "I want *no alarms.*" To the tellers: "I want *drawers open.* I want *money stacked.* I want *no alarms.*" Pointing to the vault behind the officers, he said, "You see that vault there? I want that vault cleaned of cash in three minutes. *You,* and *you,* will clean that vault of cash in three minutes. Begin *now.* All others in this area: on your hands and knees, crawl immediately to the tellers' area over here to my right. Move *now. Hands and knees.*" As tellers, officers and customers began doing as they'd been told, he chanted at five-second intervals: "I want *no alarms,* I want *no marked bills.* I want *no alarms,* I want *no marked bills.*"

The money was coming out. James wanted to check the clock above the tellers' area, but knew better. He watched the guard's face as he moved slowly around the desk to accomplish the man's disarming. And the face was scary. It was smooth and framed with silver hair and absolutely crimson. The grey, nearly white eyes were sightless—he was having some kind of fit, perhaps.

Burris felt his was the hardest job—to watch helplessly from the car.

For the first moments after James had drawn out on the guard, only James and Bill Junior were visible to Burris. And then Dwight came up from the rear of the establishment, herding together some people and putting them down onto the floor, holding aloft the German machine pistol like something he wanted to keep above a rising flood.

The scene appeared to Burris as a moving diagram flattened out against the window, a vision revealing the weak spots in their plan. It was a big bank. As Dwight moved forward, Bill Houston was left to secure nearly half its area by himself. James's firepower was nullified; he was useless until the guard could be disarmed. In the recesses of the place, where Burris's vision couldn't penetrate, men were cleaning the vault virtually without supervision. Burris had been prepared to endure unexpected calamity—a cop might arrive to cash his paycheck, a self-armed citizen might open fire in defense of his savings—but to witness how tenuous was their command of the bank and its customers, to know that almost any degree of resistance would be uncontainable, would ruin everything, would plunge them into chaos—it made him want to run inside and start shooting people. It was fake! This was bunko! They were bluffing here, they intended to create an impression of strength and get away with money by intimidation. We're not going to make it, he thought. We can't handle the least go-wrong. Save myself, save myself. This is crazy!

And now their operation *did* in fact appear to be going crazy. He heard popping noises from inside the bank and saw James, coming around behind the guard's desk to take his gun, abruptly moving backwards, as if jerked by the belt. The guard was standing up now, and because of the elevation of his desk—designed to give him a sweeping view of the bank, to make him the most powerful figure in it—he seemed taller than a natural man. In his hand he held a black revolver, and the expression on his face was definite and clear to Burris as he fired again, wounding James somewhere in his abdomen. His face was tight and pale, almost the color of his silver hair. James fell backward, and Burris could no longer find his brother in the view.

And then the guard seemed not to know what came next. He only stood there. Dwight was looking over his own right shoulder, in an attempt to keep secure the area behind the tellers' windows. And Burris could *feel* them hitting the buttons in there, could *feel* the silent hammering tremor of alarms moving under the world and up his legs.

The guard posed in his bewilderment like wax.

Burris was out of his seat and unaware of it, standing next to the car's open door, an unarmed bandit wearing a false beard on the sidewalk before a bank. *"Somebody kill that motherfucker,"* he screamed.

"Kill that son of a bitch," Burris screamed.

His brother was down. He cried from the pit of righteousness, *"Kill that man!"*

And Bill Houston did.

Now that the shooting was started, Bill Houston wanted it to go on forever. Holding his gun out toward the guard and firing was something like spraying paint—trying to get every spot covered. He wanted to make sure that no life was showing through. He didn't want the guard to have any life left with which he might rise up and kill Bill Houston in return. When the guard was still, lying there at the open mouth of his C-shaped desk with his jaw hanging off to one side and the blood running down his neck and also back into his hair and his ear, Bill shot him twice more in his chest, and would have emptied the shotgun into the guard but caught himself up short, feeling he didn't want to spend his shells, because shells were more precious than all the money that surrounded them now. The smoke of gunfire lay in sheets along the air around his head, where light played off the fountain's pond and gave it brilliance. In the center of his heart, the tension of a lifetime dissolved into honey. He heard nothing above the ringing in his ears.

As Jamie steered James's pickup—borrowed a little bit ago, she couldn't have said exactly when—the experience was like that of piloting a boat. The back wheels seemed unconnected to the front. The heat of late morning strewed the asphalt with imaginary liquids, and the world seemed out of synch with itself. She had the black transistor radio going on the dashboard, its muttering and snickering generally submerged in the noises of traffic. Everything was turning to rubber in her hands.

Standing on the seat, hanging onto the windowsill with one hand and the dashboard with the other, Miranda looked to Jamie just like a little baby doll from Paradise in a new dress from Marshall's, a discount establishment. Miranda was singing a little song: "I gotta go, I gotta go, I gotta go," and after a while, as if by singing these words she had made them come true, an urgency crept into her voice and then she was no longer singing but had set up a chant—"Mom I gotta go-do-tha *bath*-roo*mom* I gotta go-do-tha *bath*-roo*mom* I gotta—"

"Hush, fer Godsakes," Jamie said, and just then very clearly the transistor on the dash said, "Only twenty more days." An electric shock of fear ran down her legs. "I gotta go too," she said.

They were right downtown, on what she believed was a one-way street. At the outermost periphery of her vision, she glimpsed some flowers drifting down like rain when she turned her head to find a parking space. "I hafta go now, right away, because I can't wait," Miranda informed her desperately. As if it had just come to life, Jamie felt the deep throbbing of the truck's engine all around them, and beyond that, the pounding of summer heat so deep their human ears were helpless to place it, the pulse of thought, of reality itself—and she braked swiftly, overcome by a sense that the next moment of time meant everything. Softly the radio spoke to her: "Call 248-SAVE." "Oh my God," Jamie said, and tears sprang up in her eyes. "Stay here," she told Miranda, and got out of the car.

"Mama!" Miranda said, frightened, hopping up and down on the seat.

"Stay here!" Jamie told her through the window. She left the car in the street. Just inside a restaurant there was a payphone. In her jeans were three dimes, and she put all three in the phone and pushed the buttons: 248-SAVE. "Phoenix Pool-it," they said when they answered.

"This is Jamie," she said. Her mouth was sticky with dread.

"Jamie?" they said. Then, "Well—hi, Jamie. What can we do for you?"

Sweat made the receiver crackle against her ear. Her breath came in gasps. "Got a message for me?" she said finally.

"Uh—message?" the voice asked. There was a neutral dial-tone helpfulness to it, the unresisting dead tenor of machine. "I'm not sure I understand, Jamie."

She hung up, her head stinging with embarrassment. She noticed that the graffiti on the walls around her was written in another language, in strange letters resembling pyramids and swastikas—she couldn't make any of it out, but one or two things seemed to say "Oh my God!" and "Oh my God!"

"I'm almost going in my pants!" Tears stained Miranda's new dress when Jamie got back into the truck and pulled away swiftly, refusing to glance back even once. Only a half block up was a blank space of curb that might have accommodated several vehicles. Jamie leaned across Miranda and opened her door for her before getting out herself. "Hey," she said to a man in a green janitor's outfit, "tell me where there's a bathroom, will you?"

The man, an Indian with bloodshot eyes, the whites of them almost as dark as his flesh, gestured behind him with his cigaret at the building they fronted. "Maybe right inside here, huh?" he said. Jamie hauled her daughter by the hand up the concrete steps and inside.

It was the police station. Jamie's thoughts were like this: wo-wo-wo. They were all around her, and everything was brand new. Her blouse was sticking to her back. A few people and policemen were here and there, but the place seemed empty. The spacious room expanded and shrank imperceptibly. She kept pushing it all away from her face by a conscious effort of her mind.

In an area behind the front counter, a uniformed man examined white and yellow papers. He acknowledged Jamie with a nod and looked at her. "What's up?" She became aware of radar on her skin. His face was a shimmering computerized wall of beef.

In a sudden act of surrender, wanting only to divest herself of shame, she said. "I don't know." She felt she was confessing everything.

Miranda said, "I wanna go to the *bath*room." The cop stood up, and he was a small man. He peered over the counter at Miranda and laughed. "One more second!" he said, pointing the way. "Twenty more feet!"

Jamie followed her daughter into the ladies' room and entered the stall right next to hers. She dropped her shorts and panties and sat down feeling safe, safe, safe—locked in the john, in the bowels of the police—and she realized all at once what a strain her bladder had been experiencing. It seemed she would never be done. She noticed she was jiggling both her feet, clenching and unclenching her jaw until her head ached. Boy, if this ain't the very edge of it all, I just don't know, she thought. The noise of her stream beneath her drifted near and away. For a couple of seconds it was as if she were only remembering it, as a person might who'd recently died—she decided to forget about shopping and concentrate on getting home now, on getting past the police —and she could hear some words in the sound of water, faint voices prowling the limit of her ability to keep a grip.

On his way into the darkness of the movies, Burris bought a plastic cup filled with popcorn. There was no possibility he would eat any of it, but he wanted to appear to know what he was doing. It was midafternoon, and he was terrified.

Dim bulbs in sheer wells overhead cast down a little light on the rows of seats where, in all the theater, no more than a handful of patrons waited patiently for the end of the film—all of them men, none of them accompanied, although one person toward the front talked out loud to himself as if that were company enough. It was a sorrowful and ostentatious pre-war theater. Burris sensed rather than saw the pointless curtains dripping as if putrefied from the walls, as he waited at the top of the aisle to trust his eyes. The seat he chose, in the very front row, shrieked as he sat down in it. Without thinking he put his hand in the popcorn, and right away he was nauseated by the greasy feel of it. Putting it aside, he took a bottle of Jack Daniels from his back pants pocket and stared forward in total blindness at the screen, taking a pull from the bottle every ten seconds or so until half of it was gone. Around him men choked and coughed, and the one man talked, explaining to the darkness that no worthless bitch of a whore would ever tempt him to get himself chopped into pieces by some halfbreed. Then he stopped talking.

On the screen, two men fought with knives in a western barroom.

Burris understood none of it for the moment. His throat hurt, and the pulse in his head was enormous. The air-conditioned theater seemed too cold, but just as soon as he noticed the chill, he started to perspire. His throat ached more and more—it was as if a tennis ball had caught itself in his Adam's apple and was swelling inexorably—and then suddenly, great sobs burst out of his lungs. He bent over in his seat, crying and coughing, and saliva found its way into his sinuses and burned his eyes and nose. The tears streamed over his cheeks. Trying to hold back sobs, he produced a squeaking sound. The crowd in the barroom on the movie screen shouted and exclaimed incoherently, while behind him, the men in the theater kept their silence.

In a minute he sat back in his seat and let the light from the screen play over him, greatly relieved and calmed. But he didn't know what to do—he could never again see anybody who knew him, and every stranger was a hazard—and he understood he'd be caught. Almost as soon as it had passed he could feel, deep in the recesses of itself, his panic being born again. His face was hot and cold. A tingling sensation passed through his arms and legs, as if they were coming awake. He gulped the bottle empty, and nearly vomited. Wearing long trenchcoats, carrying shotguns and rifles, men on horses rode along a dirt road, passed into a forest, and made for a cabin in the clearing. Burris wished he could engage himself in their story—a story of men with guns, exactly like his own, except that nobody going to the movies ever guessed the essential, gigantic truth of it, which was that these men would trade everything they had for one clear minute of peace.

As he stared slack-jawed at the screen, almost overcome by the whiskey, his eyes abruptly turned gruesome and his stomach began clawing at itself. Trying to look like nobody in a hurry, nobody worth looking at or remembering, he rushed to the foul john and sat, nauseated and quaking, on one of the two stools there.

Burris wanted to weep with frustration because the lavatory was cramped and filled with stink, and the stalls, in one of which he sat chilly and vulnerable with his pants around his ankles and his arms around his belly, were without doors. His bowels moved with a spasm that shook him, and he began feeling better. Maybe no one would come in, while he sat like this in his utter helplessness. He felt that men who owned themselves and who had nothing to fear, coming into the bathroom to relieve themselves, would attribute all the odors to him alone.

But nobody was around, and there was nothing to distract him from himself but the drawings of genitalia and the urgent, depraved messages scratched on the walls that hemmed him in. At this moment, the vision of Burris's spirit was riveted on the single fact he could be certain of: he was a wasted and desperate human being who hated himself. Anyone who came to stand before him at this moment would see the person Burris Houston as he really was—finally naked, finally made clear. Above all, he knew he would be caught. He would be arrested and harmed. He only wished they'd get to it. From his shirt pocket he took a ballpoint pen, a cheap one that wouldn't write properly, and on the partition to his left he slowly wrote:

Ill suck your cock mmmmm

Underneath it he wrote:

When   Put dat and time

And beneath that:

Fuck You Homos

He thought he heard someone coming and hastily used the toilet paper and pulled up his pants, though he feared another intestinal spasm. Half-drunk and yet with fear racing throughout his system, he looked at himself in the mirror and saw nothing. There was nobody there. He left quickly. The next movie they were going to show was *Coma,* and he didn't want to miss any of it.

But the story of the grim and terrible events in the lives of armed bandits was still playing across the screen when he sat down, and it was far from finished.

He'd seen this movie before, it seemed to him, on TV: driven to desperate measures by their status as renegades following the Civil War, the James brothers of Missouri led a life of fighting and hiding. They were the first to rob trains. The backwoods people they'd grown up among protected them from authority. What had become of that time when a person could depend on his neighbors?

Burris could identify with these men. Once they'd made the initial move over the line of the law, everything else followed with the certainty of a boulder travelling down a hill, picking up wreckage in its path until an awful landslide of people, places, and things slaughtered you in a confusion of blood. And what could you do about it? You couldn't expect the James boys to go looking for employment, hunted as they were like animals by the FBI, or whoever it was—the Pinkertons, Burris heard them called now—and so, in the end, although they were older and probably didn't care any more about the Civil War, probably felt no anger against their enemies, probably wanted nothing more than to ride and hunt and live and breathe in the woods of their childhood, in the bosom of their families, in the company of their friends, they were driven nevertheless to strike as bandits once again. As the six gang members rode feeling like lords of the land into the tcwn of Northfield, Minnesota, everything started to go wrong. The teller in the bank claimed he couldn't open the vault, and in a hypnotic moment of anger and chaos, somebody shot his face off for him; and the people of the town of Northfield, it now turned out, had arranged themselves everywhere—behind barrels, on the wooden roofs, under the water troughs—to ambush the brothers and their comrades as they stepped out of the doors of the bank. From one end of the street to the other, the men faced nothing but the firepower of hideous strangers. Burris had never seen anything more horrifying. What he couldn't understand was why people who didn't know you, people who'd never even seen you before, could be so filled with hatred they would risk their lives to see you die—why the bank guard had risen up, his eyes two white mirrors of terror, to rip apart poor James Houston with a gunshot wound, throwing himself away forever in the effort.

Burris didn't know why he'd left his brothers. It hadn't been a conscious choice. One minute he'd been standing on the sidewalk, and then almost simultaneously, it seemed, he was walking away from the Chrysler along the edge of the dry Salt River.

Burris felt his throat swelling again and knew he was about to weep; but the James gang, slowly and mercilessly ravaged as they charged through a mutilating swarm of bullets, back and forth, driven like a pack of wolves, thwarted at either end of the dirt street by barricaded murderous citizens, did not know anything about sorrow, grief, or fear. Methodically they ranged up and down the town's thoroughfare, seeking an opening for escape, increasingly decimated, picking up their wounded when they fell from their horses, risking everything, absolutely everything, to take their brothers home. Holding his jaw tightly shut, the tears burning up his face in the dark theater full of lonely men, Burris understood at last that whatever the odds, whatever the chances, whatever the outcome and regardless of what came down, these sons of bitches did not intend to take any shit. They did not take shit, and they did not give out: and they never, ever turned each other in.

It didn't seem to Burris now that he had a body at all—he'd been invisible to himself in the bathroom mirror, he could scarcely feel himself inhabiting his own clothes—because the world of events had changed him from a person into a story. He was one of the Houston boys: bastard son of the murderer H. C. Sandover, brother of the killer Bill Houston. He was somebody he could never have imagined, member of a clan joined more deeply than the blood. You can do whatever you want to us, he thought; but you can't pretend like we never lived. It came over him that everything surrounding him in the darkness was fake, and that only he was true, the front of his body bathed in light from the tortured screen, where the James brothers abandoned their bleeding comrades in the forest and took themselves empty-handed into a future of assassination and imprisonment: a future exactly like the past.

In an acre of space, hundreds of machines competing to drown the head in sound made a noise as immense and palpable as silence. The meetings and partings of tens of thousands of empty plastic bottles gave the building the clattering atmospherics of a feverish, underwater bowling alley that stretched forever in any direction and yet was contained within itself—which was, as Burris understood it, the condition of the universe. In such a storm of sound the ears lost consciousness. No one spoke save during breaks, when the machines were alarming in their metal sleep and the necessity to shout wasn't felt. And yet, when the machines were running, any worker was able to hear small, other noises within the general clamor of industry. On line number six, adjacent to Burris's line, a woman who was privileged to smoke big cigars and play the radio while working kept her disintegrating Sony tuned to golden oldies all night long, and Burris heard these songs clearly as if by a sixth sense, in a way not quite like hearing, but more like knowing.

Either they were coming for him or they weren't.

He was the hopper loader for line number five. A forklift brought him a skid stacked with four hundred eighty cardboard boxes, each box holding twelve empty plastic bottles. With a razor blade he cut the strings that held the massive bundle together. He lifted and upended each box, spilling the contents into a larger cardboard box, until he'd emptied eight boxes and the larger one was full. The use of this larger receptacle saved him from having to repeat eight times the next and most important part of his job, which was to stand on tiptoe, lifting the box above his head, and tumble ninety-six empty bottles into the hopper. In a sea of noise the cigar-smoking lady's radio played "Louie Louie." Burris adjusted his movements to the tempo.

At the hopper's base a mountain of a woman sat by its smaller mouth where the white anonymous bottles drooled onto the conveyor belt before her, and she set the bottles upright on the belt two at a time. For months she and Burris had worked in partnership, attending to these ministrations, but because of the noise and the woman's personal ugliness, he had never had a wish to speak to her. She was a stoop-shouldered old woman whose face seemed fashioned by a child from dough, puffy and wearing a single expression of permanent grim sorrow.

Burris stacked on top of one another the eight cardboard boxes he'd emptied, and then, as the bottles moved beneath the silk screens down the line, he pushed the stack around to the end of the conveyor belt, where a black youth with his hair tied up in tiny bunches packed the bottles, now printed with labels and instructions, back into these boxes they'd arrived in nine or ten minutes earlier. Near him an old man with a scarred face, skinny and tense and proud to work quickly, arranged the packed boxes into bundles of four hundred eighty, fastened them all together with steel bands, and waved with authority while a forklift, its operator ignoring his gestures, carried the boxes out of the building to waiting trucks and ultimately to the bathrooms and kitchens of the nation. Burris hated this old man, because Burris hated this work and the old man seemed to prize it.

Today he was at his job because he couldn't think of anywhere else to be. He was a little drunk and he had no more money for movies.

He wore a teeshirt and cut-offs, that the authorities might see he was unarmed.

Lunch in thirty minutes, and he felt the power and grace of a man working well under the influence of amphetamines bartered for in the men's room at shift-change. He turned, lifted, spilled shapes; turned, lifted, spilled shapes. The incredible noise owned everything, but he was in it, a part of it, turning, lifting, spilling, a denizen of this turbulent mechanical flood. The larger box was full. He turned, grasped, hoisted, and raised it, spilling shapes into the hopper. The double doors to the building were open, and in the square of white light they admitted he could see squad cars coming to a halt. "Like a Rolling Stone" was playing on the cigar lady's radio, and Burris was a part of that, too, and it was all a gigantic maelstrom from which escaped tiny bottle-shapes into the waters of American daily life. Something in his inner ear— more known than heard—was saying *Burris, Burris* as he turned, lifted, spilled: an officer, leveling a riot gun at Burris's chest. The officer's mouth was erupting in his flushed face, and *Burris, Burris Houston* was known within Burris. *As you stare into the vackyoom, of his eyes* was also known, and as he walked away from it all dressed in terror the radio was letting him know, *How does it feel. Tell me how does it feel.*

5

On the first day Bill Houston stayed on his back in the lower bunk and failed to know whether he was awake or sleeping. He became involved in his mind with red squares and triangles.

On the second day he woke to a curious sensation and found that his left hand, trailing over the edge of his bunk, was adrift in water. Christ Jesus save me. They're doing it to us. We'll all be drowned.

The bars, tinted a pale institutional green, might not have been there at all. The spaces between them might have been colorless panels affixed to green air.

He gripped the upper bunk's edge and hoisted upright. The

queries and exclamations from neighboring cells gave him to understand there was trouble with the building's pipes. He removed his socks—his shoes had been taken from him, and his shirt—and waded two steps through a three-inch tide to the combination toilet-and-sink. As he approached the wall there, and the mirror—a circle of polished metal welded above the sink at the end of his cell—he knew he travelled the last small distance of a journey he'd undertaken to complete a very long time ago. And now it was finished. And now another was beginning.

He was alone here, one of the special captives isolated because they were believed capable of great violence. His head ached from the back of the neck through the cranium and down the bridge of his nose: in the mirror he saw that both his eyes had been blackened. Bruises circled his belly below the ribs. More than anything at this juncture, more than innocence, liberty, or another chance, he wished for a drink of Seagram's Seven and Seven-Up. Then he thought of drinking it with friendly strangers amid a place of calm: a barroom of polished oaken tables and imitation leather stools. The chest-fever of his need broke in his throat; before he could tell if he was crying tears, he turned on the faucet and splashed his face.

Crouching over the water, he looked before him at rivets studding the metal wall, their green heads flaking to bare primer the color of cherries. The sink was spilling over. Dizziness circled his vision, and he leaned on the basin and rested his knee on the metal toilet that jutted left from the same clogged pipe that served the sink.

The noise of heavy shoes and the cries of prisoners, the screech of buckets on the catwalk, the whanging of steel gates, the slosh of water against bulkheads—men swearing and ruining mops against iron bars—all of this was so like the atmosphere of a large seagoing vessel that the two experiences, penal and naval, blended for a moment in Bill Houston's perception and he tried to cling to the idea that he might only be assigned temporarily below decks.

In Pearl Harbor he'd wandered once through a destroyer in drydock—the choked and baking *Somerville,* out of San Diego— and loose inside it, he'd been deeply alienated from its haunted stationary silence, its failure to live by moving. That afternoon he'd been a trespasser in a forbidden sepulchre, a sailor on a ship on dry land, helpless to travel or float or do anything but walk away on two legs, leaving whatever errand had brought him to that place unaccomplished. And now he felt the same, but he couldn't depart. They had him this time. After this time there would be no other.

When the guards came to make him presentable and bring him out temporarily among free people, he refused the razor they offered. "It's your face," the fat guard said, and handed him a shirt, and the other fat guard gave him back his boots. They were both fat. They flanked him enormously as the three of them proceeded along the gauntlet of cages to the control unit of A-wing of the Maricopa County Jail's main building. The prisoners they passed were silent, casting their gazes to the right or left of Bill Houston, but all attended his passage with a frozen zeal that they could hardly disguise and that he had never witnessed in any men anywhere. "I stepped in some shit this time, didn't I?" he told the guards. He was perspiring in the mechanically refrigerated air, and he wanted them to fool around a little, the way guards always fooled around. But they were alarmed, too, by the uniform ice-quiet of men who normally reacted with vocal interest and derision to their comings and goings, and so they kept quiet themselves.

They took him handcuffed through doors and corridors into a pre-war section of the building which smelled of fresh paint, and then down a hallway strewn with dropcloths and stepladders. The painters working there said hello and chatted with the guards as they passed. It eased Bill Houston's mind to know that in some circles he remained anonymous. When they ushered him into a spacious conference room still in the midst of its remodeling, where two overhead fans revolved wearily in the ceiling and a workman's radio played softly, he looked at his lawyer for the first time. It was the same lawyer Bill Houston had always been saddled with—about five-six, round glasses and mustache, western string tie, a public defender looking twelve or thirteen and clutching a plastic briefcase with probably nothing inside of it. Bill Houston sat down across the table from him and said, "I can't get up no confidence in you."

"If you could afford fancy counsel, you wouldn't be here," the lawyer said. "I'm assuming that. I'm assuming you're a person who doesn't like to kill people. I'm assuming you wanted money and that you didn't want blood. I'm assuming you're not homicidal."

"I'm not," Bill Houston said. "We didn't mean it."

"That's what we're going to convince the jury of. We're going to convince them you're stupid and tragic, but basically a nice guy."

"How's my brother?"

"Which one?"

"There ain't but one involved here. James."

"James is alive. He may need more surgery later. Burris is now involved. He's in custody, too, over in the Annex, and so is a man named Dwight David Snow. Nobody wanted to talk to me, but my guess is probably James gave them up."

"No way." Bill Houston shut his jaw tightly against a sudden feeling he might cry in front of his lawyer.

"He was hurt pretty badly, William."

"Can we cop a plea or something? What's your name?"

The lawyer looked tired. "I'm Samuel Fredericks, known to everyone as Fred. Or, actually," he admitted, "as Freddy." He looked tired even of his name. "The prosecution is offering you this deal: You agree to plead guilty to first-degree murder, and they'll agree to do everything they can to execute you. The Assistant DA says it's almost like going free."

"Shit," Bill Houston said. "Does it hurt?"

"What?"

"Does it hurt. The gas." Bill Houston laid his head down on his arms and felt a misery descending that made him want to puke. "If it don't hurt, I'll do it." With a tentative tongue he tasted the metal of the conference table. To hear himself say "the gas" was wrenching. He was living somebody else's life, some murderer's. "Does it hurt?"

"You can't imagine," Fred said.

Across the run was some fellow who stayed in his cell's top bunk —though nobody occupied the lower one—with his right arm flung across his eyes and the fingers of the left examining, one by one and continually until he slept, the rivets in the ceiling above his face. Bill Houston spent a great amount of his own time leaning against the bars of his cell, his own arms hanging out into the catwalk area as though he breathed through them the air of relative freedom; and he watched this man. He didn't want to lie down because on his back he was defenseless against his thoughts —the fear that he would confront a door opening onto a gallery of faces, the loved ones of the man he had killed. That he would walk amid a crowd of officials, normal people who knew how to live their lives. He would be made to look on the dead face of his victim. He had a feeling he was going to find out something terrible about himself, something even worse than that he was a murderer, something so essentially true as to be completely unbelievable. He dreamed of witnesses. The twisted relatives behind the glass—the more they tormented him, the more viv-

141

idly they themselves were agonized, and he could never pay anybody the price. It wasn't the punishment that hurt—it was the punishment's failure to be enough. These visions and comprehensions were no less present when he stood embracing the vertical bars of his cell, but they seemed less actual then, less likely to happen, as if by butting up against what kept him from walking freely in the world, he came to know what kept him safe from the future.

The motionlessness of his defeated neighbor across the run drove Bill Houston to activity. He walked the cell and sometimes exploded into grunting bouts of calisthenics that left him exhausted and temporarily serene. He petitioned for a pen and pad, and when his thoughts turned to Jamie he let them burn a message—three or four words a day, he was no scholar—into the page:

Seperation is painfull. I still think of you everyday. There was a flood here it was on the 2nd day after they got me— Later everybody found out it was 2 cooks—they did it on purpose & screwed up the drains in the kitchen—Hey I hope you get a chance to tell everybody Im sorry. This is beng delivered by Freddy my lawyer. Im glad James didn't die.

I have feelings for you you know its hard to say—Tell Burris no hard feelings, it could of been anybody.

Seperation is painfull. But who knows of hopes of tomorrow? Maybe we'll meet again some sunny day Jamey.

> *Love*
> *Wm Houston Jr*
> *Tell Burris hell still be my brother*

· · ·

"I've been informed that, contrary to your request, you cannot be moved any closer to the television on A-wing," Fredericks told him. "The TV is for men serving sentences. You haven't been classified, you're violent, etcetera etcetera. No TV."

"Okay," Bill Houston said. "Don't make no never-mind to me. In the joint I'll get enough TV to where it makes me sick."

Fredericks held Bill Houston's communication in the palm of his hand. "I'll try and get this delivered. But I think you should know Jamie's in the hospital."

"What happened? She all right, or what?" Fredericks had brought him Camels, and he lit one casually. He didn't want his true concerns identified by these people.

"She's in the hospital," Fredericks said. "I don't know the details. She had a nervous breakdown of some kind."

"Got a little frazzled, hey?"

Fredericks looked at him curiously until Houston said, "What about the kids?"

"I don't know about the kids. I didn't know there were any kids. I presume any kids would be taken care of."

"Okay. Anyway," he said, shoving the ashtray across the table toward Fredericks. "How's James?" But Fredericks didn't smoke.

"James is recuperating nicely. He's doing just fine. And I think we're going to get your trials separated after all, because Dwight Snow's got some slick counsel with pull. He's off on his own."

"Off on his own?"

"He's getting a change of venue. Separate trial in another county. He's in a good position—no record, and he was in possession of an unfired weapon."

"Bastard held off till I had to go in," Bill Houston said.

"I did not hear you say that."

"I got nothing to hide." One he'd learned from Jamie.

"Anyway, James's gun had been fired, but he claims he just hadn't cleaned it and just hadn't loaded it fully."

"That's true. I don't remember him firing no rounds."

"They *may* try you together, but they're beginning to see how it could get messy. And Burris I can definitely separate—his position is already more clearly defined than Dwight Snow's."

Bill Houston said, "I don't understand any of this. Just bring me comic books and cigarets. I give up."

"Well, I'm talking strategy. And that strategy is designed to keep you alive. I wanted you all tried separately, but I don't know now. We may want you and James to go in together. I really can't pretend to have anything figured out till I get the prosecution to loosen up a little. The thing is," he said, and stopped Bill Houston's hand from fidgeting, covering it with his own, "everybody's being very weird over at the DA's. I'm just starting to suspect that whatever they want, our policy should be to want the opposite. No cooperation."

Bill Houston stripped the paper from his cigaret butt. Both men observed the small movements of his thick fingers raptly, until he'd added its tobacco to the contents of his county-issued plastic bag of makings and dusted the last few grains from his fingertips. "Couldn't you try again? I mean, you know, to get them to move me down closer to where the TV is at?"

Fredericks swept the ashtray and his briefcase from the table with a deft violent movement of his arm; the two guards—the same two who went everywhere with Houston outside his cell—came to attention, but did not draw near.

The expression on the lawyer's face said nothing about how he might be feeling. His tone of voice was identical to the tone he always took with the defendant. "You're miserable, William. You're the complete twenty-five cent desert crook. You're without any sense of personal responsibility, even for your own life. But I'm going to save your ass."

"Hey, this intimidation shit—you don't scare me."

"That's good," the lawyer said, "because when your lungs turn red, I wouldn't want you to be scared. I wouldn't want you to be scared when your soul goes up the pipe."

Angels

Bill Houston sat with his feet out and crossed, staring at his boots, and said it one more time out of a thousand. In his cell he said it silently to the walls, and in his sleep he cried it out loud and woke the others in neighboring chambers: "I killed him."

She was greatly aware of the wide thirsty grounds of the place surrounding these slow interiors, but nothing of that outer world was available to the sight of inmates because the windows were so high. Their ties cast crisscross shadows along the floor this morning, so that as Jamie entered carrying newly issued toilet articles, her feet, in disposable paper slippers, passed through quadrangles of light.

Along opposite sides of the ward ran two rows of eight beds each, most wearing comfortable green or red plaid bedspreads. Lamp fixtures encased in wire mesh disrupted the walls of pale yellow, which were bare except for a small sign near the door that said:

TODAY IS

tues june 4

YOUR DAY

A couple of elderly women sat on a bed playing with cards and a board full of pegs, and another old woman with a leathery face walked up and down between the rows. These and the few others present wore wrinkled cotton gowns identical to Jamie's. On the bare mattress of the bed the nurse pointed her to, there were two women seated side by side like passengers. They looked all right to Jamie, but they were smaller than your regular women, and one of them had a face caked white with make-up and made horrible by a thick smear of crimson lipstick—she looked like a voodoo doll —and as Jamie approached, the other one began making sounds no human should have been capable of. The doll-lady nodded and said, "She means the President." The other kept making awful noises and the doll-lady said, "Too fast, Allie—slow down!" To Jamie she said, "The Department of Money, she means."

Now Jamie saw that the woman held to the folds of skin around her throat one of those mechanical buzz-boxes for people without a voice. The matter being discussed excited her tremendously, and she gestured even with the hand that held the box, waving it around unawares so that it spewed noise inconsequentially. Her friend said, "That's The Times We Live In. The Times We Live In, she's saying."

"Excuse me," Jamie offered, "you got your fat ass on my bed."

The nurse came out of the bath-and-shower room at the end of the row of beds, carrying a stack of bedding for Jamie. "Alice, is this your bed? Is this Bridget's bed? Bridget—is this your bed?"

Alice placed the voice-box against her throat and said, "Fungyoo."

"Alice," the nurse said. She seemed about to smile.

"Zlud."

"She means Slut," her companion said to Jamie.

"Off the bed, please." Throwing the bedding down beside them on the mattress, the nurse made shooing motions with her two hands.

The women got up simultaneously. "Nurses do it with all the doctors," the doll-faced woman explained to Jamie.

"Nuns do it with priests," Jamie agreed.

The two went one direction, and the nurse went the other, but she paused at the door two beds away. "You can have all the milk you want."

"I what?"

"On account of your stomach, hon. Doctor Wrigley put it on the orders."

She sat on the bed and put the toes of one foot on the instep of the other.

"Do you want some milk?"

"Sure—what are you so hot about this milk for? Something in it?"

"Okay, hon," the nurse said. "We'll talk about it later."

She lay crossways on the bed, pillowing her head on the folded bedding and putting her feet out flat on the floor. An odor of honeysuckle came vividly to her nostrils, floating on the warm dark air of Wheeling, and a gust of the steel mills' breath. Her entire childhood lay immediately outside this place of walls, if she could only get to it by changing into a thing of hours—because she was understanding things now, understanding about time, about its directions and how to change the way of it, and about the many things that were happening moment by moment unbeknownst to the forest of blind dead human shapes, the forest of wooden men—

"What are you supposed to be?"

Jamie sat up. On the edge of the adjacent bed sat a blond and emaciated woman no older than herself.

"We're on the Mamie Eisenhower ward," the woman told her. She wore the standard washed-grey cotton gown, but she'd covered the sleeves, and the front of it, with secret writing.

"I'm under observation," Jamie said. But an understanding of what this meant temporarily eluded her. She rested her elbows on her knees, her head and hair drooping forward. The design of the floor was six-by-six inch square grey patches with a little copper crown in the dead center of each one.

The woman said nothing. She scratched herself between her legs with the obliviousness of a child. She was thinly beautiful, but her teeth were as yellow as her hair, and tiny blue veins showed around her temples. She appeared in need of fixing. She looked broken and thrown away. Jamie said. "So what's your story? I mean, what are you supposed to be here for?"

"Me?" the woman said. "I'm nuts." She began laughing; laughter that sounded like: ratatatata. Jamie liked her, but at the same time she wanted to slap the woman's face.

She woke from a Thorazine unconsciousness because someone was yelling, *"Sergeant!"* The ceiling was far away, then inches above her face, and then properly positioned. *"Sergeant!"* She raised up in bed. It was daytime. The large woman with her hair all chopped off, who always wore a man's blue boxer shorts instead of a gown, was talking to the nurse. Her face was crimson, her eyes pink. Two male orderlies in white stood a yard back, respectfully, at her either side. "I want to see the Sergeant!" the woman insisted. "Do you know where we are?" the nurse said. "The Sergeant's not here. There isn't any Sergeant here." All the patients were quiet and shiny-eyed, watching this exchange. The big woman put her hands on her hips and began to huff uncontrollably, working her jaw as if trying desperately to dislodge something from her throat. One of the orderlies took her in a hammerlock from behind, and the woman lifted him clear off the floor, his legs dangling like a child's. The other man wrapped his arms around the two of them, and they all three waltzed monstrously toward the Quiet Room, a chamber made completely of tiny tiles with a drain in the center of its floor.

The bed on her left was empty and silver in the darkness, its bedspread thrown back. Jamie was the only one awake to hear the cries. The old woman who slept there next to her was trudging heavily up and down the aisle between the two rows of beds, and at the far end she was silhouetted against the light from the bathroom, a bent figure of helplessness with her hair in a bun. Several afterimages trailed her in Jamie's sight, and Jamie shook her head violently but they wouldn't clear away. The old woman seemed to be carrying something close to her belly. "I lost my Catherine! I lost my Catherine," she cried in a voice as unstopped and mournfully low as a foghorn's. Jamie had to shut her eyes a minute, because the bathroom light made them burn. When she came awake again, there were curtains full of light drawn around the next bed, and moving human shapes silhouetted on the curtains. They muttered and conspired in there below the level of her hearing—a black form hurriedly approaching and entering said, "We've got to catheterize her," and the other shapes said softly, "Catheterize, catheterize, catheterize." Jamie began to shake uncontrollably. She couldn't find her voice to scream. She turned to the right, as if to summon help from the lumps of unconscious and insane people in their beds. When she tried to blink the handfuls of warm sand from her vision, everything changed and it was morning. The old woman was sitting up in the next bed, looking at the pages of a magazine.

"Volleyball, you guys," Nurse Helen said.

"Volleyball?" Jamie said, looking at Sally for confirmation.

Sally appeared too starved and weak for games. She lay back on her bed and pulled a fall of her blond hair over her blue-veined face, going into some kind of trance. Volleyball.

"Raphael!" Nurse Helen sang.

"Do I have to go and play volleyball?" Jamie asked her. Last night, until dawn, screams had come out of the tiled Quiet Room. She couldn't put these screams together in her mind with volleyball.

"Doctor Wrigley doesn't have you down for sports," Helen

said, and looked up at Raphael, the stocky Chicano orderly, who was just approaching. "She doesn't like volleyball," Nurse Helen said, gesturing at Sally on the bed. Together they took Sally— Raphael by the feet, Nurse Helen by the hands—and carried her like a sack from the ward. Sally began laughing, and they did, too.

In a minute the nurse was back, breathing hard. "Hey," Jamie said, "are we supposed to be crazy, or what? How come people have to play volleyball when they're supposed to be crazy?"

"Physical activity's important, Jamie. And I don't like the word crazy. You're sick people trying to get well. This is a hospital, right?"

Jamie could feel the back of her neck getting tight again. She knew it was a hospital, for God's sake.

"I think you should play volleyball, too. I'll talk to the doctor about it Monday when he comes in."

Jamie felt angry, because she didn't want them to figure out that she wanted to play volleyball. She was flustered. She wanted to be out there right now. Why didn't the nurse just tell her to play volleyball right now?

"Matter of fact," Nurse Helen said, "if you want to, why don't you go out there now? Always room for one more."

"Are you shitting me?" Jamie cried. "Who told you to say that?" She was all pins and needles. She took hold of her own head with both hands. "They're reading me! What did you do to me?" The enormity of her situation pressed in against her. She didn't want to face it.

She stood on the bed, balancing with difficulty there, and pointed a finger at Nurse Helen. She wanted to explain something important, but the only word she could think of was, "Ya! Ya! Ya! Ya!"

Raphael came in. Some boy in a doctor's smock came in. She was completely enraged that they thought it necessary to hold her down and give her a shot. Nerves popped in her skull, voices chanted incomprehensibly, and the event accelerated into a white smear.

The doctor sat on her bed with his legs crossed one over the other —a new doctor, one she hadn't met before. "Just what are we talking about here?" she said.

"Well," the doctor said, "essentially we're talking about anything you want to talk about. Anything that concerns you, anything that bothers you right now. Do you want a cup of coffee?"

"Coffee?" she said. "Why are you trying to give me coffee? I'm coughing enough as it *is*. I have tuberculosis," she told him, "that's why I lost all this weight."

"Okay then, let me ask you a few questions. Can you tell me the day and the date, Jamie?"

"It's the fifteenth of whenever, nineteen hundred and fuck-all. You think I don't see through that one?"

"Maybe you see through it, but I'm not trying to fool you. The date is right on the wall." He pointed at a sign on the wall that said:

TODAY IS

thurs june 27

YOUR DAY

"My only reason for asking is to find out if you take an interest in what day it is. Can you tell me where we are today, Jamie?"

"We're in the goddamn looney bin."

"Can you tell me the name of the hospital?"

"Arizona State Hospital."

"Great. Very good. Now—please don't object to my asking you these very obvious questions, okay? Just trying to get our bearings. So how about telling me what wing of the hospital we're in right now?"

"Wing? You mean, like of a bird? Of a dove? 'The Wings of a Dove?' "

"No, that's not quite what I mean. I'm asking you to tell me the name of this part of the hospital. All the parts are named after famous people."

"The parts?" For a second—just a tick—she saw something breaking out of the doctor's face. "I don't know who you are, Mister," she said, "but if you don't get out of here you're finished." A weasel or something.

"I'm knocked up, is what I think," Jamie kept telling them. Her stomach churned continually, and it was a rare moment when she came around to the true state of things long enough to appreciate that it was fear, a pure utter terror created by her thoughts, that took hold of her innards and squeezed until she was nauseated. "You've got to get yourself organized on a daily basis," the nurse told her in confidential tones. "Well, fuck you," Jamie said. She was sorry to talk this way, but it was necessary. You only had to listen to the news to see that the world was splitting apart. She had no idea what was going to break out of the middle of things when the time was finally at hand.

The temperature in the lock-up was uniform. Only by watching those who came and went could he believe the desert summer's heat had arrived. It blazed in the faces of new arrivals and melted from the pores of the guards as they greeted him at the start of each shift—always the first of their duties, checking the prize defendant at the end of the cellblock. And as the temperature rose out in the world, Bill Houston felt the jaws of his captivity crushing him, and found reason, in the news that Fredericks brought him twice weekly, to count himself among the lost.

"We have a grave situation here," the lawyer said. "I was misinformed earlier, and I misinformed you. This Crowell—the man who was killed in the hold-up—they're calling him a cop. He wasn't a cop. He was retired. But they're just not looking at that fact. They want to get technical.

"I won't sit here and quote every law for you, but I'll get you Xeroxes of every statute they're charging you under, and you can look at them, along with any other statute that applies, including death penalty statutes, William, because that's what we're looking at. These bastards want you. I'm not going to pretend they don't want you, because they do." He watched Bill Houston as if Houston might now offer some sign that none of it was true.

The defendant made a gesture of invitation with his hands: play on.

"What I'm saying is we've got a nice new judicially acceptable, constitutional, unbeatable death penalty statute, and there's this huge groundswell all of a sudden—but I mean everybody, all the powers-that-be—I'm telling you they want to off the first killer who comes down the road, without *any* delays—that's you, William—and they also intend to gas the oldest remaining denizen of Death Row out there in Florence, who happens to be Richard Clay Wilson, the child-murderer. I really can't believe that *they* really believe they can bring all this about. But they're like kids. They've got this new law and now somebody's got to die."

By June's end it was clear that Burris, James, and Bill would all be tried—separately—according to the original schedule. Bill Houston had been identified unanimously in a line-up. And now the lawyer was helpless and nervous most of the time. Houston knew lawyers; he knew when a lawyer had lost. None of their motions for delay was granted. There was a fearsome, inexorable gist to the decisions. Always the Ninth Circuit ruled against Fredericks, his motions to quash evidence, to have witnesses impeached or testimony thrown out. Houston's trial approached unimpeded, as if no defense whatever had been mounted against it. "We're going to send you over to have your head checked," Fredericks told his client. "But I guarantee you right now, they're going to certify you sane."

The new man across the catwalk, an Italian sort of guy who'd beaten his father-in-law mercilessly and broken a great many of his bones, asked Bill Houston how it was going. Bill told him the truth: "I'm going up the pipe."

"Let's walk Irene down to the Outpatient Area for her appointment," the nurse would say—this nurse or that nurse, she really didn't care which nurse.

"Let's walk over to the commissary," the nurse would say. "We can't have you lying on that bed all day, thinking those thoughts of yours."

"Do you know where you are?" the nurse would say. "It's July Fourth. This is the Helen Keller ward."

She was right about lying on the bed. When Jamie was up and doing, things were okay, but when she lay down and considered the way of the world, her picture of life came up shining impossibly, with a molten border around it, and she knew that things were not at all as they had seemed, that it wasn't July Fourth, that the boiling slimy whores had a grip on the march of time and that everything was happening over and over. She heard the instructions coming out of the walls, affirming that she must kill herself in order to save the others, to get the days going again, and she experienced her own murder at every turn of her breath, repeatedly born into the blazing frame of a moment that never changed. Often she woke up in a place made entirely of green and white squares going away from her infinitely. For a moment, once, she had a handle on the whole situation: this was a small room of tiles with a drain in its floor, and she'd been asleep on a little pad almost like a quilt. But in a minute, it just wasn't like that at all. It was much, much more horrible. Everything depended on the position of a single green square, and she didn't know which one, but the certainty with which her heart seized this one, then this one, then another—it was driving her insane. Her mouth was chapped, and both arms were sore. When they opened the door to the little room and came in with the hypodermic—the nurse and the little monkey-man who told her what to do—she remembered about her arms.

"Well!" the nurse said, as if that said it all. "Did you remember that today you're moving over to the Madame Curie wing?" She knew how to make the sheet of the bed float softly.

"What?" Jamie was watching her make the bed.

"Moving day! Oh—" the nurse was disappointed. "You don't have your things together. Where's your stuff, honey? Your toothbrush, and your little diary?"

"Here's what I think," Jamie said. "Everybody fuck everybody up the ass. I mean—oh, eat everything made of shit. You cunt whore suck." She could feel her face getting hot.

"You're going to have to watch that mouth," the nurse said.

Jamie decided to say Cunt Whore Suck one thousand times, starting now.

"Okay, Sister," the nurse said. "Over to the Curie wing for you. And if you don't get straight you'll end up over in the Mathilda wing."

"The Middle of Things?" Jamie said. "I'll kill you!"

"Lane! Raphael!" The orderlies appeared, and the nurse told Jamie, "You're going downhill. You're on that slickety-slide."

"I put a spell of a curse on you!" Jamie said.

The nurse said something that sounded like Voodoo Dissolve, and as Lane and Raphael carried Jamie along by her arms, she shouted, "Did you call me Voodoo Dissolve? Did you? Did you?"

She moved from the Curie wing down to the Joan of Arc ward toward the end of July. All the walls were made of tile here, and the floors, too, and there were drains in the floors at intervals the length of sixty-seven tiles. Two of the drains were sixty-eight tiles apart. But she could never be sure. Nothing was ever definite, and once she was done counting anything, if she wanted to know how many, she had to count again. And although the drains stayed the same and the main hall was always eight hundred twenty tiles long, she had to be sure, she couldn't be sure, she had to count again. She knew the lie was inside of a number. At the very center of one of these numbers, where it was supposed to be nothing, where it was supposed to be only a thought, there was a speck of dirt in your eye.

Whenever they brought her back from the place where they attached her to the wires, she saw the same thing on the wall as they passed by, a picture of herself, a message about her fate, beseeching her to prepare: a bright poster, a whirling orange child-style stick figure on a maroon background under the inscription: *If You Catch Fire,* DROP AND ROLL . . . In the middle of the night they raped the woman in the bed next to hers. Jamie's ears roared at the inside of her head as she watched them pull the dividers eagerly around her. People hurried to and fro in the night, carrying pieces of the woman into the bathroom and eating them; in the morning there was nothing left of her.

Scarlet light and white heat awoke her. She was in flames.

The bed rocked on a momentary ocean, and then came to rest in the dark hospital ward. It was not her clothing, but her flesh itself that was burning. The light that came from her splashed shadows on the walls and floor that shifted and changed their minds about what they were, as she leaped out of the bed, stood still a minute at the foot of it, and then was torn up the middle by the agony of her personal heat. *"I'm on fire!"* She dropped to the floor and began rolling and whirling. Everybody in the room burst into laughter. There were red lights, and sirens. She couldn't breathe because of the smoke that filled her lungs like water. It *was* water, they were trying to put her out—but she was burning. It *wasn't* water. They were urinating on her profusely. They all had huge floppy shoes. They were clowns, they threw her in a monstrous tub with a drain.

Beneath her the tiles rippled and breathed. The pulpy surfaces of the walls ripened uncontrollably under her observation, inhaling endlessly like lungs preparing to blast her face with a calling or a message. Stripes and pyramids fell across the air in nearly comprehensible organization, writing that changed just before she understood it, and the room itself became a vast insinuation, swollen with filthy significance. She wanted to catch her breath and wail, but realized that her own lungs were already full. When she exhaled, the room seem relieved of its tension momentarily: she was crushed to remember that this very same action of ballooning and diminishing had been linked to all her other breaths. This terrible, terrible thing that was happening was her breathing.

The beat of things, their steady direction, had dissolved into nothing—this room wasn't happening then, it isn't happening now; maybe it's a dream of what's going to happen or what will happen never. The sound of her own voice injures her like a shock of electricity through her ears, but screaming herself to hoarse exhaustion is the only reprieve from breathing.

She looked up out of her voice and saw the angel.

He will have ears like a cartoon of organic growth. He is yellow with light but covered with mobile shadows, animated tattoos. His face kept changing. His voice will come from far off, like a train's. His body is steady and beautiful and hairless, the wings white, incinerating, and pure, but the head changes rapidly—the head of an eagle, a goat, an insect, a mouse, a sheep with spiraling horns that turn and lengthen almost imperceptibly—and the entire message had no words. The entire message will be only the beat and direction of time. Yes is Now.

The angel who says, "It's time."

"Is it time?" she asked. "Does it hurt?" He will have the most beautiful face she has ever seen.

"Oh, babe." The angel starts to cry. "You can't imagine," he said.

Bill Houston was in the State Hospital having his sanity questioned. From his high-security room he looked out over fifty meters of parched grass to a low wall of stone topped by hacked and complicated wrought-iron, and beyond that to the intersection of two streets, something he hadn't expected to have so prolonged an opportunity of examining ever in his life again.

He stood at the wire-mesh window with his arms crossed before his chest. He wanted to tear himself away from the view and think a minute about something important—about Jamie, who was here in this hospital somewhere, and he wished her peace; or about how to convince these people he was crazy, incapable of telling right from wrong—but he really only wanted to look down at the ordinary street seized by the dusk.

Each time he swallowed, he gulped down half a speech. Things to be said roiled in his belly, washed by acid, but he was silenced by his own confusion as it compared to the stately transactions of the casual street. He understood that he would be executed and deceased, that everything he saw would outlast him. Solitary now for weeks, he'd taken to speaking directly to the heart of the moment, fearing everything, repetitively and increasingly convinced that he would soon break apart and be revealed, be destroyed, be born. He recognized it as an old feeling that came and went, but now it came and stayed. He lived alone and thought alone. The nature of murder made him alone inside himself; he'd never been so alone.

I did it, he said to the gas station outside. I'm ready, let's go. I can handle the pain, but I can't hack the fear.

He watched Twenty-Fourth Street all night, all the doings there, the repair and refueling of cheap cars, the going and staying of prostitutes and citizens and strangers, a trickle of types up from Van Buren, people, if he could only have seen them, with motels in their eyes and a willingness to take any kind of comfort out of the dark heat. And while he paid no attention to what he feared, it happened. Slowly the time had been transformed, in the usual way that the passing of an evening transforms a street corner and a place of simple commerce there, like this gas station. And then abruptly but very gently something happened, and it was Now. The moment broke apart and he saw its face.

It was the Unmade. It was the Father. It was This Moment.

Then it ended, but it couldn't end. Now there was a world in which a man got into his blue Volkswagen, thanking the attendant as he did so, and closed its door solidly. It was a world in which one fluorescent lamp arched out over the service station, and another lay flat on the pool of water and lubricant beneath it. It was a world he might be lifted out of by a wind, but never by anything evil or thoughtless or without meaning. It was a world he could go to the gas chamber in, and die forever and never die.

There was some daylight now. He looked through wire mesh, intended to withstand the heat of a blowtorch, at a world awash in a violet peace. He felt as if his feet had found the shore. This is your eternal life. This is for *always*. This happens *once*.

They had her by the elbows, one man on either side. The door opened. Her feet didn't touch the ground. One of her slippers fell off. "End of the line, baby. Smack in the Middle of Things."

"What the fuck's fucking? Fuck you," she said.

"That's real pretty," they said. "This is the center of the Search of Destruction where the Devil will eat you."

"Going to eat your pussy. All bloody teeth," another one said.

"Fat soul. Suck warts of the soul in death. This is Ground Zero," they said.

"*Wait* a minute," Jamie said. "Wait a minute." The answer was only a word away.

"Great!" they said. "Why don't you do that? In the middle of the night."

"As soon as the Search of Destruction eats it," they said.

She felt her face getting hot. She could hardly keep a grip. "Is the bomb here?"

"You tell us," the man said. "What do you think?"

They took him up to the eighth floor of the Maricopa County Court building in handcuffs and leg irons. "Not a chance," Fredericks said as soon as he saw Bill Houston in chains. He took a breath to protest, and the prosecutor, a tall grey gentleman who appeared very wise—Bill Houston wished *he* were the defender —raised a friendly hand and nodded to the guards.

They unbound him amiably and he sat down in a pew beside his lawyer, but Fredericks wasn't satisfied. It galled him that his client should have to appear before impressionable jurors wearing the denim garb of a prisoner. He was nearly apoplectic. Houston had never seen him so excited, so wronged and abused—but he appreciated that this was the show-style appropriate to the side that could hope to triumph only in a limited way and piecemeal, through a horizonless march of writs and appeals. In future appearances William H. Houston, Jr., would be permitted to wear a cheap suit; but it would go into his brief that on the trial's opening day he'd been made to look like a criminal before the jurors who would decide his fate.

Now the jury wasn't here, however. Now only a skeleton crew of local justice was present, the stenographer laying out his equipment, three prosecutors, two jailhouse guards and two courthouse guards, and a few spectators. Bill Houston couldn't help feeling like an errant youngster when he spied his mother in the third row.

She looked small in these quarters, with their distant ceiling and ominous bulking judge's bench, their originless fluorescent illumination, their austere and holy Modern Airport decor and the posh hush of carpets and central cooling. She wore a pink dress and a pink pillbox hat with a pin in it and a veil, which she removed when she saw her son to disclose her face looking healthy and alive, just as she'd looked at his trials in the past: because it was only on these occasions when her loved ones fought the law that anybody took any notice of her. Though her kind of people were generally ignored—or at best slightly mourned and slightly pitied—by those who built and staffed these magnificent rooms, everyone was forced to see now that it was really for her kind of people that these places had been built, after all—and now *you* are working for *us*. Now you'll take reckoning of us in your sight. The last shall be first. It made her ashamed to take very much pride in all of this tragedy, and yet the day seemed electric—she had to admit it—because her boy was on page one.

He looked good. They had him dressed in work clothes, like a person of low degree, but he looked good. Obviously he'd been eating and exercising. It was the same as always. Left to his own devices, he was hopeless and dangerous both, but in custody he flourished. Her oldest son was at home in locked places.

At the very center of things they killed Jamie. It had a hold of her wrist at the very center of things, saying, "You damn doodad, you can't do that, you damn doodad, you damn doodad." There were two of it. "You smear shit on the wall, you're going to clean it up every time," it said. It took hold of her wrist and made her hand look huge. She threw her hand away and it picked her back up and attached her to her hand. She was choking. "Responsibility," it said. "Terrification."

It had a hold of her wrist and dipped her hand into the waters of the lake of poison.

The screaming of sirens came out of her two ears. Waters of the lake of the poisonous filthy death. You wanted everything. Well, I gave it to you. I'm nothing now.

"This is a clean establishment of walls," it said. "We're making you put fire on the things you've smeared on the walls."

That's me. That's what you wanted.

"Responsibility and Terrification in the Lake of Fire and of Poison," it said.

When they made her hand touch her secret writing formed from the filth of her bowels, she ceased. Greatness exploded in her face.

I have been washed away off these walls.
But this is me, she said. I'm still here.
What am I doing wrong?
Where the secret terrible word had been, there was fire running down the surface.
WHAT AM I DOING WRONG?
"That's the first sensible thing you've said this month," it said. There were two of them.
So that's it, she said, and she felt the electricity running out of her brain. There's no way out of here. This is it. I'm here forever. I had it all backwards.
Baby, they said, you are impressing the hell out of me. You see what you needed all this time? Responsibility. Self-respect. And do you know where you get that from?
Fire in the center of your name.

As the days unrolled and Bill Houston came to understand that he would never be called as a witness, he lost interest in these proceedings. He didn't trust anybody to speak in his stead—he alone knew who he was. He only wanted to be allowed to share this person with the jury. He just wanted them to know the person they were condemning—and it angered him that he should be the cause of all this show, and his mother coming day after day to watch, and they had no intention of acknowledging him. He felt like a grownup in a room full of children playing with toy cars. To get them to see who he was involved tearing them out of a tiny exclusive world of their own creation.

In his bored reveries he came back again and again to the moment when he'd turned his weapon on the bank guard. The guard had been paralyzed by the chemistry of panic and excitement, and in the instant of time when Bill Houston had tightened his grip against the trigger, he had known there was a better way of dealing with the situation. It might have been possible to disarm the man somehow and leave him alive. That space between heartbeats had been big enough to accommodate any amount of contemplation of the act. It made him feel *good,* it made him know that life was *real,* to admit that right there inside that nick of time he'd seen a clear choice and been completely himself. He wanted to confess it to these people, because he sensed there was a chance they might never hit on a moment like that one. He just wanted to give away the most important thing he knew: I did it. It was me.

He watched his trial from behind a wall of magic, considering with amazement how pulling the trigger had been hardly different —only a jot of strength, a quarter second's exertion—from not pulling the trigger. And yet it had unharnessed all of this, these men in their beautiful suits, their gold watches smoldering on their tanned wrists, speaking with great seriousness sometimes, joking with one another sometimes, gently cradling their sheafs of paper covered with all the reasons for what was going on here. And it had made a great space of nothing where Roger Crowell the bank guard had been expecting to have a life—a silence that took up most of Bill Houston's hearing. It was a word that couldn't be spoken, because nobody knew what it might have said. It was the vacuum no larger than a fist, no more spacious than the muscle of the heart, that drew things into it and unbalanced and set loose all the machinery Bill Houston saw moving around him now. They said things; they failed to say things. They stood up; they sat back down. They huddled at the judge's bench, and they conferred in his chambers, and they passed among themselves expressions and slight gestures intelligible to no one else. Periodically Fredericks drew him close to explain what deal had been struck, or how the evidence was tilting. But what Bill Houston couldn't shake was the remarkable power in the subtle difference between pulling and not pulling the trigger. A tiny movement of the finger, a closing it together of half an inch: and it caused these men and women to convene, to parade themselves mercilessly along the routes of their arguments and their laws, never omitting a proper station or taking a shorter way, as if they actually had it in their minds that they might have come here to accomplish anything but his death.

After Gate twenty, after the steel tunnel they passed through wordlessly, after the glass control booth with its computer-era panel of dials and switches and gauges, after the strip search, after the lecture, after the V-notch was cut into each boot-heel and the boots were returned to him, doors slid apart and slid shut, and he walked naked past cells accompanied by a single CB-6 guard in khaki, through the shouted conversations of men made invisible to one another by barriers. Each green door they passed was solid rather than barred, with a small window up high and left of its center. Here and there an irrelevant face peered out.

His things were on his bunk. To see that they'd been carried here and now awaited him made him feel special; they didn't provide this service for the usual run of prisoners. He inspected his new belongings for defects: a pair of yellow leather work shoes —how had they guessed his size? was it on record?—two blue cotton work shirts, two pairs of jeans—way too large, and he was glad they didn't know everything about him—four pairs of white underwear, four white teeshirts, eight white socks, two white handkerchiefs, two white towels. Handkerchiefs. When had they started giving handkerchiefs? he lay on his bunk with a teeshirt thrown over his groin and listened to the talk around him—talk of women, drugs, money, and cars. Bill Houston wasn't one to keep silent in these areas, but he couldn't find an opening when he couldn't see anybody's face. And it was different, too, that in the pauses between remarks, you couldn't say whether the conversation was over or not. Somebody might be about to speak or fallen fast asleep, and you couldn't tell. It was like talking on the telephone, but no one ever said "Hello," or "Goodbye."

He was where he'd been heading for a long time. He was unconscious before they turned the lights out.

The sun was just high enough to get over the east wall. The small exercise yard of CB-6, which had been primarily in shadow, now showed a bright slash of glare in its westernmost corner. There were only seven or eight men out, and a couple of guards. Bill Houston recognized H. C. Sandover across the court, bending over something on the ground in the company of two other men.

Because the guard nearest them seemed edgy, watching a clump of murderers in which any plot imaginable might now be taking shape, Bill Houston stayed where he was, in the sun. In his third day here, he was still getting used to the high-resolution planes and angles. Something about the black of shadow, the tan of desert buildings, and the brutal whiteness of the light made Bill Houston think of Spanish missions, of Mexico, of things that were definite and clear. There was that quality to this place—light and silence; things that lasted slowly.

The guard was nearer the three prisoners now, almost among them, and they were all sharing a joke.

Bill Houston went over, and H.C. squinted up at him, taking his attention from a large toad he was fooling with. His blond hair had grown shoulder-length and grey. He wore small round glasses tinted bright blue, and a red bandana tied pirate-style over his scalp, almost like a hat, though hats were forbidden. "Got us a news service going here, Billy!" he said.

The guard said, "That frog isn't about to go nowhere, friends."

"What do you think, Billy?" H.C. said. "He had to get in, hadn't he? My whole philosophy of life is hanging on this. I believe in a reality behind circumstantial evidence. If he knows a way in, he knows a way out." H.C. turned the toad over, still squatting, something like a toad himself, on the ground. "Circumstantial evidence is what got me here." The toad was bigger than a man's fist and must have weighed half a pound. "We can attach a message for your Mom, Billy," H.C. said, standing up, and he was as tall as Bill Houston. Somehow the other two men had disappeared. The guard had taken up a stance some few feet away.

"Mom was real anxious for me to say Hi."

"It's been almost six years since I've seen the woman, Billy. Over half a decade."

"Just the same," Bill Houston said.

"That's one twentieth of a century. Do I have to tell you that people get kind of blurry?"

"How come you never write her?"

"I don't need to write her. She writes me."

"I don't mean nothing by it." Bill Houston was trying to make peace. "I'm just, you know—"

"—just relaying the greeting whereby she puts a little guilt-ride down on my list for the day, right? Some things get blurry, Billy, and some things get real sharp, real clear." Bill Houston could feel a heat greater than the day's coming off his stepfather. They'd never shared much more than a dwelling, but now he wanted to say something about how much he'd always resented this man. Before he could find any words, H.C. said, "God, you stink."

"What?"

"You make me sick just like poison. I smell cyanide gas all over you, Billy."

"The last person to call me Billy was you."

"I'm gone." As if with great purpose, H.C. moved across the

court to the weights area, where he gazed down upon a long-haired Indian who lay on his back on the bench in the sun, pressing nearly two hundred pounds above his face. When the Indian began to struggle and the weights to waver, H.C. put one finger under the bar and helped him to raise it the last go. Bill Houston wished, if somebody had to be murdered by him, it could have been H.C. You still got the fastest mouth in six states. You made my mother kiss your ass. He sensed, standing here in the court with the heat climbing over the walls as morning became noon, how all the circumstances had tangled themselves around his head and made him blind; how things were so confused he'd never even begun to think about them, never been able to see how, in general, his life made him feel terrible, and his mother's life, and all the people he knew. But now it was plain to him, because suddenly he had a vision of everybody in this prison yard rising up out of the husk of himself, out of his life, and floating away. And what remained was trash.

Oh man, it must be a hundred and twenty degrees in this place. He could feel the heat against his eardrums, and behind his eyes. He shook his head to clear it, but things were already unbearably sharp and clear.

Just as she thought of hospitals as places of permanent death, Mrs. Houston was accustomed to equate the Phoenix Sky Harbor with blackness and tragedy—with the tearing apart of families, with the movement of stunned hearts through twisted worlds, with the last sight of the faces of people who would never return. And the Sky Harbor was like that now, nightmarish and alien—the plane to take Miranda and Baby Ellen away would leave at 3:45 AM—but it was also physically very different from the old Sky Harbor, which had been more like a bus station than a center of international flight. In the new Sky Harbor there were three separate terminals, and a huge multi-level parking lot that nobody would ever have found their way through but for the paths of green paint drawn across the shiny concrete, and arrows and signs that swore these many paths led to various elevators that would carry them to innumerable airlines; so that deciphering these messages and following these arrows and abandoning herself to this strange journey through incomprehensible structures with Miranda and the baby and Stevie and Jeanine began, for Mrs. Houston, to take on spiritual overtones.

When they found themselves delivered onto an escalator that was drawing them up some seventy or eighty feet toward a gigantic mosaic Phoenix bird rising up out of its ashes, she understood what it would be like to stand before the doors of Heaven, and knew how small a thing was an earthly life.

She held Miranda's hand, and also carried the child's brand new plaid suitcase. Miranda was silent for now, cowed by their surroundings and a little stupefied because she'd been sleeping in the truck during the ride over from Stevie's. But a waxing alertness communicated itself through her tiny hand, as she sensed the nearness of toys and candy and doodads for sale to weary travellers. Mrs. Houston tightened her hold.

"Maybe tomorrow's paper's already out," Stevie said. She held Baby Ellen against her belly in a Snugli, a kind of reverse knapsack for infants that Mrs. Houston had never seen the like of before. "There's something new every day," Stevie said, but she wasn't talking about a Snugli, she was talking about the Houston Gang in the papers. Her eyes wore the pink and bruise of grief. Anyone could see she'd been destroyed by all this.

But it was happening for the third or fourth time to Mrs. Houston, and she bore it well. "It'd be today's paper now," she said. "It's already three o'clock Thursday morning." Turning to speak to her daughter-in-law, she fell to looking over Jeanine, the last of them in line on the slowly moving escalator. Jeanine looked like a young starlet heading for the cameras, very tanned and clear-eyed in her sleeveless white party dress. She did not carry the big blue *Urantia Book* tonight. She was about to become a Hertz Rent A Car girl in San Francisco.

As they stepped off the escalator and took their bearings, Stevie unzipped the baby's travelling bag and made certain everything was inside it. "Just give her a bottle around four-thirty— or whenever she wants one, if she really starts bawling. There's an extra one, too. And some Pampers, but you won't have to change her, probably. There's some Gerber's beets in there." She handed Jeanine the blue canvas bag. "She loves those beets."

"You mean four-thirty our time, or four-thirty their time?" Jeanine said.

"It's the same time, honey."

"It's California," Jeanine said. "It's a whole different zone."

"Not in the summer," Mrs. Houston said, "'cause we're not on the Daylight time. We're on God's time."

"How am I going to recognize their dad?" Jeanine asked.

"I guess he'll recognize them, won't he?" Stevie said.

They were approaching the entrance to the flight gates and security area—its conveyor belts and austere efficiency and X-ray eyes. Mrs. Houston ignored a wave of apprehension that she'd be tortured. "Here's one," Stevie said, and stepped over to an all-night gift shop and bought a newspaper. "There's something new every day," she explained to no one.

"It's always on page one or page two of the local section," Mrs. Houston said. Still holding Miranda's hand, she maneuvered around behind her daughter-in-law, who held the paper out at arm's length and tried to read over Baby Ellen's head. Ellen was awake and alert, and appeared to be trying to strike Stevie across the cheek with a rubber pacifier she gripped stiffly in her left hand. "Transferred to the Death House," Mrs. Houston read out loud. "I can't believe it." She turned to Jeanine. "I won't believe this is the will of God."

"I don't know. Nothing makes sense," Jeanine told her.

"As of tomorrow, he won't be in CB-6 no more," Mrs. Houston said. "They're going to have him in the Death House, in some kind of waiting room. Well," she said, "it's about time he learned to wait."

Instantly Stevie was angry. She shoved the paper at her mother-in-law as if jettisoning everything connected with their misfortune. "Don't you understand they intend to kill your son in two more weeks?"

Mrs. Houston was scornful of the idea. "The soul of a man don't die." She waved the newspaper around at the entire airport. "That's what this is all about."

Tears spilled from Stevie's red eyes. "Well I just want to smell him. I can't smell his fuckin' soul."

She cried for a minute while they all stood there waiting for her to stop. "I'm talking about James," she told them.

"I know," Mrs. Houston said. "But at least he ain't going up for the capital punishment. You'll see him soon as he gets well. And you'll smell him if you really want to." She looked down at Miranda, who was tugging on her hand and saying, Mizz Houston, Mizz Houston? "We're almost at the plane," she told the child. "What do you want?"

"Does it say in the papers that my mother is dead?" Miranda asked.

The three women were silent. Jeanine finally said, "What?"

"Does it tell about that she died?" Miranda repeated.

"No, honey." Jeanine was at a loss. "No—your Mom's not *dead*. She's just *resting*."

"Resting means when you're dead," Miranda informed her.

"She's resting in a hospital to get *well,* she's not resting like she's *dead,* or anything."

Miranda bunched her new dress up between her legs. "I have to go to the bathroom."

Jeanine took her into the bathroom just this side of the security area. While she waited for Miranda, she looked at herself in the mirror. Her hair was starting to grow long again, and she'd just had it permed. Her dress was white on white. She wore red lipstick. Knowing a killer had taught her that she must live.

"Stevie?" Miranda called, her voice echoing out of the stall.

"I'm not Stevie, honey. I'm Jeanine."

"Oh," Miranda said. Then she said, "Jeanine?"

"What is it?"

"Um . . ." The moment seemed to take place under water. "I'm almost done, Jeanine."

"Good," Jeanine said.

When Miranda was ready to leave, Jeanine turned on a faucet and insisted she wash her hands. Standing on tiptoe, Miranda thrust the very tips of her fingers momentarily beneath the rush of water, then stood under the electric blower letting the hot air wash over her face.

The blower ceased, and she stood there. She was wearing a white dress almost exactly like Jeanine's, and they were alone in the sudden tiled silence of an empty public place. She held out her arms to Jeanine. "Will you lift me up into the meer?"

For a beat she didn't understand.

And then she understood, and lifted the child up before the wide glass. Above the row of identical porcelain sinks that seemed to diminish into a haze of tiles, Miranda saw herself. She studied herself carefully in the mirror, turning her face this way and that within its indefatigable duplication of everything. "That's not me," she told Jeanine.

She placed her hand on the white ruffles of her own breast. "This is me."

6

Brian, the Death House three-to-eleven guard, wore the usual guard's uniform of starched khaki. But as soon as Brian, Bill Houston, and the guards transferring the prisoner had entered the small red brick building that housed the condemned in their last two weeks of life, Brian took off his shirt and never wore it again except when leaving the Death House. He kept his fatigue-style cap on his head at all times, however, and also his mirrored Air Force sunglasses, which Bill Houston knew from experience were a hindrance to clear vision and could only be a punk affectation. Plainly, for Brian, the way he looked was the beginning of the way he wanted to be. He was only twenty-three or twenty-four.

"Well," Bill Houston said, standing in the doorway of his new home with the three guards, "it ain't exactly a dungeon or any-thing."

"No," Brian said. He was a serious man and a nervous one. "It's dry in here."

Bill Houston couldn't think why the guard would speak of dryness, unless he meant to reassure him about a few spots of water here and there on the concrete floor, apparently remaining after a hosing down. On his right, through a doorway without a door, was the Waiting Room, consisting of two small cells side by side. To his left was a wide glass window through which he saw a small room like a radio station's sound-booth. This was the room for the witnesses.

Directly before him was the gas chamber, looking like nothing so much as a shabby vehicle of transport. Its heavy air-lock door stood open wide, and he regarded with a dizzy incredulity the bulky metal chair with its leather straps, while Brian whistled and removed his khaki shirt, enjoying this.

"Have a seat," Brian said. "Make yourself at home."

Bill Houston tried to laugh. But he failed.

"No—seriously. Nobody would care. You want to try it on?"

Bill Houston saw that he made this offer not simply because it was in his power to make it, but because he really believed it might be accepted.

A group of men from the yard had gathered near the entrance —men who'd been going to the clinic to sell blood plasma under the supervision of a tall guard who now stood among them hatless under the hot sun, looking almost like their prisoner. Brian talked to them with true friendliness: "Anybody want to go for a little ride today?"

The men laughed—a burst of sound like the outcry of startled game birds. It carried out over the field and echoed off the walls that dwarfed them.

Through Bill Houston there raced an impulse, which he felt

was not his alone, to say all right, sure, yes. But he said nothing. Swiftly on the heels of curiosity came the habitual yardbird fear and trembling, the knowledge that these people could get away with murder and the suspicion that they would like to try. It was the wholesale dream of these prisoners that they would be gassed to death while trapped in their cells. In their wild imaginings the borders of their confinement talked to them, and they were waiting for whatever would come, waiting for another name, waiting for giant times, waiting for the Search of Destruction. He knew a rush in his veins—he felt their need baked into these walls—and he wanted to make himself a sacrifice and his death a payment for something more than his stupid mistakes. If Brian could promise him he'd make the crucial difference for somebody, he would walk through the door and be slaughtered here and now.

He came within a yard of the opening and looked around inside the chamber. The seat of the chair rested on a cast-iron case perforated with holes to permit the escape of gas. Two straight two-inch pipes ran from directly beneath the witnesses' window and into the base of perforated metal. He assumed these pipes fed the pellets of cyanide into their bath of acid beneath the chair. The thick leather straps for the arms and legs were plainly darkened by the sweat of those who had preceded him here.

He was wordless, and when it became obvious that he had nothing to report to them of what it was like to stand here condemned, the other prisoners moved on toward the clinic.

The guards waited patiently for Bill Houston, and Bill Houston stood waiting patiently to be terrified by the means of his death, which was after all just a little room like a diving bell, or a cheap amusement park submarine ride, with a large wheel on its door for screwing it tightly shut. He just felt obligated to experience more than mild interest. But the sight failed to move him until he saw the stethoscope—one with an unusually long tube—built into the door. He comprehended that the shiny flat end of this listening device would be attached to his chest after he was strapped in, and it just didn't seem fair to him. It meant he wouldn't be allowed to wear a shirt, he'd be half naked before strangers—and now it came over him vividly that his death would be attended, observed, and monitored by people who couldn't appreciate how much he wanted to live. They would probably think, because he offered no resistance, that all of this was all right with him. But it wasn't. They just didn't know him. They were strangers.

He peered around at the other side of the door, the side he wouldn't see after they closed it, and was disgusted to see the stethoscope's rabbit ears dangling there helplessly. It wasn't all right with him at all!—that somebody would be hooked up to him while he was dying. It wasn't all right that a doctor would hear his pulse accelerate in the heart's increasing frenzy to feed him with airless drained impotent blood, until the major arteries burst. And all the while, this doctor would probably be wishing he'd hurry up.

But he thought of how he'd wanted to cover the bank guard Crowell with death, like paint, until no dangerous rays of life were shining out of him. I got this coming. He moved his trigger finger slightly. That's all it took. And now it's my turn under the wheel.

"What's that supposed to mean?" he asked Brian. Over the small window cut into the door, on the inside, ran a semicircular line of words in Old English lettering, something to read while the hydrocyanic gas swirled up toward your nostrils: Death Is The Mother Of Beauty.

"I don't know what it means," Brian said. "I guess you'll find out, won't you?"

But Bill Houston already knew.

.   .   .

"You wouldn't believe how good this stuff tastes," he told Brian, as he ate Wonder Bread with margarine-flavored lard on it and anonymous reconstituted soup. "That's what that sign on the door is trying to say." He gestured with his plastic spoon. "When you only got two weeks coming at you, a shit sandwich would be just fine. Even a shit sandwich without no bread."

Brian took off his cap and rubbed his head all over briskly. He was thin and handsome with short light hair and a big Adam's apple that made him look like the country boy he was. He didn't smoke, and he claimed not to drink whiskey. "They'll never get me dirty in here," he had told Bill Houston that afternoon. "They fired twenty-three dirty staff two months back. But I'll never go —you can't corrupt me. I don't have any vices you can get a pry into, if you understand what I mean."

"I ain't trying to corrupt you," Bill Houston said.

"Well don't bother trying, is what I'm getting at."

"Are you religious?" Bill Houston asked.

"Of course I'm religious. Everybody's religious in the Death House. The way I see it, we were meant to be here together at the end of your time."

"Well," Bill Houston said, "yeah." And he did agree. But he was embarrassed to say so.

The Death House was not air-conditioned. Against regulations, Brian left the Waiting Room door open to catch the breeze and presented Bill Houston with a meager view of some dirt and a stretch of concrete wall. Somebody had planted a twenty-foot row of as yet unidentifiable vegetation along the wall's base, and Bill Houston watched all day without any real interest to see if the person would come along sometime and water it, but nobody came. On the other side of the wall was the prison's medium security South Unit, and farther south than that was the self-contained maximum security Cellblock Six, where he'd spent only nine days before his transfer to the Waiting Room.

At sundown, just before the stars came out, the sky went deep blue and the yards and buildings seemed as yellow as butter under sodium arc-lamps. The air cooled swiftly, but the walls stayed hot for a while into the darkness, and the generous loops of razor-barbed wire coiled atop them were the last things to catch any daylight. The desert outside was asleep: it was the time when the animals of the day took shelter, and the animals of the night kept hidden a little longer. Across the highway to the north, the Department of Corrections' fields of alfalfa breathed green heat into space. If it wasn't peace, still it wasn't war. The prisoners had eaten their dinners and were quiet. Those serving sentences of a comprehensible length could blacken another day.

After a while an energy came out of the dark, a tin-foil singing of wind over the walls. The animals of the night set out. Inside, the TVs got louder and more lights came on. Voices were raised, and in lowered voices bargains were struck, and transactions took place among confederates. Prisoners or not, people had to make a living.

In his new quarters Bill Houston felt closer to the prison's life —closer to being in circulation—than he had in CB-6, which shared nothing, not even a kitchen, with the rest of Florence Prison. But he knew he was no part of that life, and never would be again. James would eventually come into it, and Burris might, too. Bill Houston felt sorry for himself tonight. All he could do was talk to Foster, the wheezy old suppertime guard, or taste the air. He'd never noticed before that the air had a flavor to it. It had a taste. It tasted wonderful.

That he might spend only three weeks in prison now seemed one of the worst parts of his punishment. It was inside the level, uniform dailiness of these surroundings that the wonder of life assailed him. Minute changes in the desert air, the gradual angling of supposedly fixed shadows along the dirt as the seasons changed, the slow overturn of all the familiar people around him—they spoke of a benevolent plot at the heart of things never to stay the same. But on the streets events jumped their lanes. Everything turned inside out, flew back in his face, left him wide-eyed but asleep. He'd never known himself on the streets. It was here at the impossible core of his own accursedness that they were introduced.

In this version he laid the bouquet of flowers disguising the Remington on the check-writing counter and suddenly had a thought. "Hold it, Dwight"—quietly; nobody took any particular notice.

Dwight, up by the desks, was confused. He came forward. "What is it, Bill?"

"I just think we better hold off."

"Well, we'll hold off, then. But what's the trouble, Bill?"

"Dwight, I have an uneasy feeling about today. Can you trust me on it?"

"I can if I have to. And I think I have to, Bill. Why don't we come back and try tomorrow?"

"Let me make a suggestion," Bill Houston said in this version. "Let's come back when a different guard is on duty. I have an uneasy feeling about the guard."

"I don't want to come back tomorrow," Bill Houston said in another version. "I don't want to come back ever again. I have a chance at a pretty good life—a woman, a couple of kids. There's no sense me being here. I haven't been appreciating all the gifts surrounding me."

. . .

"Neither have I, Bill," Dwight agreed in another version.

"Neither have I," James said.

"Neither have I," Burris said.

"Neither have I," Jamie said.

Things hummed, and things trembled. But things held. She wore a pink skirt and a black teeshirt. It was wonderful to feel panty-hose against her skin. But the tennis shoes made her feel like a shopping bag lady.

"About how much alcohol—what was it? Wine?" the Welfare lady asked.

"Yes. That's right. Wine." Dr. Wrigley was looking at his charts attached to a clipboard. In this situation, he was Jamie's champion.

"How much wine did you drink daily, on the average, let's say," the Welfare lady asked.

"I had it down to a real regular thing there," Jamie told the assembled officials. "I did away with the most of a half-gallon of purple wine ever night. Then I had the rest for breakfast."

Everybody nodded. There were four of them around the conference table with her. They took notes.

"And the drugs?" This question came from a small woman who was also a doctor. Jamie liked her because she seemed to be on Jamie's side, and because she wore tennis shoes. "Can you tell us what kind, or about how much?"

"There was nothing regular about that," Jamie said. "I just took every opportunity that came along to get as ripped as possible."

"How are you feeling today?" the Welfare lady asked.

"Nervous," Jamie said.

Nervous was the wrong word. She could see that instantly.

"I mean, I have my problems," she said, "but I don't think this is the Empire State Building, or anything like that."

They shifted in their seats.

"You're just nervous about being here," Dr. Wrigley said.

"You got it," Jamie said.

Everybody nodded. When she said the wrong thing, the bodies shifted. When she said the right thing, the heads went up and down.

Dr. Wrigley wasn't the only man with a chart. There was another, Dr. Benvenuto, who flipped his pages and said, "Jamie, what do you see yourself doing ten years from now?"

She closed her eyes and it came before her like a vision. "I'll be watching a color TV and smoking a Winston-brand cigaret."

That made their heads go up and down wildly. They loved that one.

"My two girls, they'll be right in the next room. Miranda'll be going on sixteen, she'd probably be talking on the phone. Got a boyfriend on the other end." She was definitely putting it all in the proper slot now—four happy faces surrounded her. "Ellen would be ten, right? She's—playing the piano. Practicing on a few tunes for the big debut thing, I guess. The recital." She looked into their smiles, and beyond their smiles, she looked into their homes. "That's what I want. A piano, a vase with flowers inside of it. A little economy car. A regular kind of life."

She lit a cigaret. "Everything would be organized into monthly payments."

Oops.

"I mean, all my current debts and stuff."

"We understand," Dr. Wrigley said, and the other guy, Dr. Benvenuto of the Outpatient Program, actually laughed.

Back in the Express Lane. She backed up a space in her head

and saw the room as one sheer piece, all of itself. Actually, they were all on her side here. They were all giving her the signals: This Way Out.

When the Welfare lady and the lady doctor with the tennis shoes had gone, Dr. Wrigley stayed behind and introduced her to Dr. Benvenuto. "I think you belong in the Drug and Alcohol Rehab program," Dr. Benvenuto said right away.

"On an outpatient basis," Dr. Wrigley said.

"Out," she said. "I love the sound of that word."

"You've got a long way to go—I hope you understand that," Dr. Benvenuto said.

"I'll take it on an inch-by-inch basis," Jamie said.

"Are you willing to do whatever's necessary to stay away from chemicals?"

"You could cut off my arms and legs."

"We don't have to go quite that far. Would you be willing to live in a halfway house, and go to a daily therapy group? Would you agree to a urinalysis every three days?"

"I'll do anything. Where do I sign?"

"It doesn't involve signing," Dr. Benvenuto said. "It involves living. That's a little tougher."

Jamie read the message several times. It was hard to get a fix on it with Dr. Wrigley standing by the bed. It was her first communication of a personal nature from the outside world—although actually it had come from another Inside World.

She felt that her reaction would be important. Dr. Wrigley had come to deliver it to her himself.

"How far back in the summer was it, when he wrote this?" she asked him.

"I believe it was right after his arrest. Sorry it took so long, but I guess you can understand."

"Oh yeah," she said. "No problem. I was just wondering." She read it again:

Seperation is painfull. I still think of you everyday. There was a flood here it was on the 2nd day after they got me— Later everybody found out it was 2 cooks—they did it on purpose & screwed up the drains in the kitchen—Hey I hope you get a chance to tell everybody Im sorry. This is beng delivered by Freddy my lawyer. Im glad James didn't die

I have feelings for you you know its hard to say—Tell Burris no hard feelings, it could of been anybody.

Seperation is painfull. But who knows of hopes of tomorrow? Maybe we'll meet again some sunny day Jamey.

> *Love*
> *Wm Houston Jr*
> *Tell Burris hell still be my brother*

"He says, 'Tell Burris he'll still be my brother.' "
"Well—if that's what he says," Dr. Wrigley said.
She gave it a little thought. "I think that would be just lovely."

When Brian came back from his supper, he was lugging a stack of newspapers and was accompanied by the two guards from CB-6. They had Richard Clay Wilson in tow. Everybody was silent. This person had killed children. There was no kidding around, and nobody offered him a try in the gas chamber's bulky chair.

Wilson took up residence in the adjoining cell with self-conscious efficiency, putting a large battery-operated stereophonic radio on his shelf space, turning it up full blast, and staring at Bill Houston with innocent menace through the noise and through the bars that separated their quarters. Bill Houston's short stay on CB-6 had given him no opportunity of meeting Wilson, but he looked hardly different from the youthful pictures Houston had seen in the papers years before. He was skinny and black, but not very black—half Jamaican and half white—with an extremely wide, flat nose and a terrible complexion: freckles and blackheads across his nose and cheeks, and irritated pores where he shaved. He threw his blue workshirt on his bunk, standing with his hands on his hips and staring them all down—casually administered gestures designed to establish him as an entity rather than a punk. Superimposed over each of his nipples he wore a tattooed cross, with lines indicating light radiating from them. He had been on Death Row, and then its successor CB-6, for a little more than thirteen years. He was thirty-one years old.

They introduced themselves to each other as Richard Clay Wilson and William H. Houston, Jr. These were the names they'd been given by the newspapers.

"We might as well get along," Bill Houston said.

"We might as well," Richard said, and gratefully plugged in a set of earphones and placed them over his head.

"Never saw nobody come down to the gas-house so fast," Richard told him, as they taped up pages of old newspapers to shield themselves from each other.

"My lawyer told me it's a new era we're entering," Bill Houston said.

"Nobody been down here for six year. I was never down here before."

"Who came over?"

"A white biker gentleman name Mavis. He got back home to CB-6 in two days."

"They want my ass. They want yours, too," Bill Houston said.

"I am the oldest and you are the youngest on CB-6," Richard said. He seemed to have a habit of suddenly puffing himself up, like a lecturer.

Bill Houston thought the man was a fool. He started to put up the paper faster. "Well, we're going to go up the pipe," he insisted.

"You for real, boy? Nobody go up that pipe no more. That pipe don't *work*. Shit."

"This time it's different," Bill Houston promised him. "I can feel it."

"You can't feel nothing. You just a baby."

"I'm a damn sight older than you are, Richard."

"Shit. This my home. You just a baby in my home."

"CROSSVADER!"

Bill Houston came up out of a dream of fields. Right; three AM.

"CROSSVADERRRRRRR!"

The guard—Houston didn't know him, had been sleeping at shift-change—was nobody; just the moving circle of a flashlight like ice in his eyes. "Next door," Houston said to the light.

"TAKE IT BACK TAKE IT BACK TAKE IT BACK . . ."

The guard shone his light into the other prisoner's quarters. Against the layer of newsprint taped up between their cells, Bill Houston saw the changing shadows of bars and the deformed silhouette of Richard Clay Wilson, the famous Negro child-murderer. He appeared to be down on the concrete floor, on his knees—

"*CROSSVADER!*" he screamed.

Now the flashlight held still, trained upon him in his cell.

"*CROSSVADER!*"

"What the *fuck* is shaking *down?*" the guard cried softly.

"It's kind of like praying," Bill Houston said.

"*TAKE IT BACK! CROSSVADER! TAKE IT BACK!*"

"Wilson!" the guard shouted, waving the light and stirring the shadows around. "Wilson!"

"Did it every single night, over in CB-6," Houston said. "But I never heard it up close before."

"*CROSSVADER! TAKE BACK YOUR SUICIDE!*"

"Well, nobody told me." The invisible guard sounded miffed. "What's he saying?"

"It's like his prayer, man. Every night, three AM. Crossvader Take Back Your Suicide."

"Crossvader take back your suicide?"

"*CROSSVADER!*" Wilson screamed. Saliva spilled out of his cries. The rawness of his throat was audible. "*TAKE BACK YOUR SUICIDE!*"

"What the hell is he talking about?"

Bill Houston said, "He's talking about Jesus, supposably. How about cutting that light out? What say we all get a little sleep?"

"*CROSSVADERRRRRR!*"

"Well hell," the guard said, "if you can sleep, I can sleep."

"He'll be done in a minute. You ain't supposed to sleep anyways."

The guard cut out the light. For a moment the dark was a soft blanket over Bill Houston's sight. And then the dim illumination of the yard lamps made a room out of it.

"*CROSSVADER!*" the murderer prayed in the black cell,

"TAKE BACK YOUR SUICIDE!" He sobbed as after a terrible beating.

Bill Houston lay in the dark with his hands behind his head, and did a little praying himself: What do you want from me? You want me to die? He thought of the hardware store clerk he'd robbed in Chicago: I made that man get down and pray.

"Crossvader . . ." He was down to the last hoarse noises he could make.

In the daylight Richard told Bill Houston, "I will not go to Jesus!" He embarrassed Bill Houston by his vehemence. "I am an alien from another planet. I was not meant to be saved."

"I admire your spunk," Bill Houston admitted.

> *"I just can't stop*
> *when my spunk get hot,"*

Richard sang—words from "Disco Inferno," most beloved of his stereo cassette tapes and one he played as often and as loudly as he himself could bear it.

Beyond rare snatches of song and his occasional speechifying, Richard by day was expressionless. His movements were at all times spacy and languid, as if he operated under an oppressive tropical torpor. What Bill Houston noticed about him early was that he never shadow-boxed, drummed his hands, or danced extemporaneously like the other blacks he'd known out on the yard. In his youth Richard had been a legendary psycho, climbing the bars like an ape, howling at the moon, crying oaths of revenge, screaming of meat and blood and sex, often going for days without sleep or rest. But isolation and a solitary intimacy with his memories had given him a shaky purchase on self-control.

A sixteen-year-old dropout, a loner, a Southside neighborhood denizen with nothing to recommend or condemn him, he'd been discovered with the hacked skeletons and dismembered bodies of four missing white children, and his lawyers had thrown him to the wolves. The general attitude on the yard toward child molesters was one of horrified despair: they were sick individuals who deserved whatever fate they might receive, and to execute them informally, by stealth, was encouraged. But the CB-6 population had mellowed toward Richard, particularly as he outlasted others who were resentenced or transferred and became the longest resident of CB-6. Bill Houston knew all about him. It was Houston's duty as a human being to hate this monster, this psychotic mutant born out of the always tragic mingling of separate races. But he was confused. He felt removed from the places where his ideas made sense. In the Death House these ideas seemed small. There was a great project taking place here—he and Richard were going to be killed—and the beat of life inside him just took his breath away and made it hard to remember why anything else mattered.

"He may not believe in Jesus, but that man is Jesus to you," Brian told Bill Houston. He was speaking right in front of Richard.

"Okay," Bill Houston said.

Richard ignored him.

"I'm not the big expert, okay?" Brian said. "But it sure seems like this, that once they do away with one of you, the other one won't have to take his ride. And there's a few people around here who agree. I'm not at liberty to say who." Brian took off his sunglasses, and to Bill Houston his eyes seemed pale and small. "So which one do you think they'd do first?" He was looking back and forth between the two cells. "Which one?" He banged the heel of his hand against Richard's bars. "Which one of you you think they'll do first, Richard?"

"Me," Richard said.

Brian shrugged. "It stands to reason. You're the decoy," he told Bill Houston.

Brian grabbed the thumb and forefinger of one hand with the other. "I'm at the doctor. He says, I gotta cut off your thumb and your finger, Mr. Cooper. They both have to go, I'm chopping them off. Oh, man, no, not my *finger*. Not my *thumb*. I go around for a couple weeks, okay?—oh, no, they're gonna cut off my finger, they're gonna cut off my thumb. I go down, the big day arrives, I'm going crazy, and just at the last minute the doc says, well, how about if we just cut off your finger? Oh, boy! Just my finger? Sure! Gladly! Get it?" he asked Bill Houston. "Doctors do that all the time. They tell you the worst. They say, we're gonna amputate two things—so you don't feel bad for the rest of your life when they just amputate one. You're the thumb. You're here for the benefit of the liberals who have to save somebody." He looked at Richard: "And you're the finger they're really gonna amputate. You're dying for William H. Houston's sins."

Richard said, "I know about engraving, you know that? Neal Harverry, the greatest forger ever, probably one of them, he was in the old Death Row and him and me receive a Federal contract making forty-five cents per hour. Seem like nothing, but it was rich back then. That gentleman taught me everything there is about forgery. I could be rich if they let me go one time. I take a week off. I take two days off—I bring you back a stack of money, Jack. I engraved a mold of stone, three feet by four feet, almost. It weighed seventy-eight pounds, they going to make a sign for a national seashore park that say: Ancient Indian Well. Corn-grinding Area. It's a map for you to look at and know where you are, and it say on there with an arrow, 'You are here.' But you ain't here." He was emphatic on this point, drilling Bill Houston with his gaze through the window in the wall of paper between them. "You are not here."

He waited for Bill Houston to form an appreciation of this fact, and then went on: "Neal Harverry said imagine about standing in the middle of a marsh in Massachusetts. Imagine about standing at the national seashore park. You be looking at that big cast-iron map. A completely stupid person. You wouldn't have no idea of the fact of a killer talking to you, telling you, 'You are here.' He said about a marsh, when the cattail plant get dry in the autumn, they sound on fire, you know, when the wind blow down on them. They crack like a battle was going on." He breathed heavily, and squirted shaving cream from an aerosol can into the palm of his hand. "You are not here," he said.

"They can't kill me because I have the poem. The poem lives forever," Richard told Bill Houston. "I connected to the creative forces on the day I wrote it."

The poem's history was known to Bill Houston. The poem had actually been written as an essay based on a letter once published in a newspaper. For most of its life it had been repeatedly plagiarized by members of the prison's community college English composition classes, and edited and revised by any number of teachers.

But if the essay had been everyone's, it was Richard who'd hit on the idea of breaking it into lines resembling verse. He hinted that he'd made many other improvements. Now in his view the poem was the child of his own creation. He kept it folded up inside a small plastic box for a stereo cassette, and it galled Bill Houston, who didn't read much, that Richard acted as if this piece of paper were better than money. From it he seemed to take much more than the pride of accomplishment. It was food and drink to Richard's ego. "I'm going to read it for my last words."

Richard lifted up his chin; Bill Houston almost gagged. "Then they'll all know bitterly that they can never kill me."

Bill Houston pretended to be interested when Richard let him read it. But he really couldn't understand why Richard insisted on personally owning this masterpiece. It didn't rhyme, and the words were plainly not Richard's—it even talked about a "nigger" —and anyone could see that somebody had typed it and then Richard had squeezed things in here and there by hand. It wasn't actually a poem: it used words of a sort that Bill Houston used himself all the time, but didn't care to see written down. He handed it back by way of Brian, because they weren't allowed to pass things directly to each other. "This is a real good poem, Richard," he said.

Brian read some of it, too, and said, "Hm! It's a work of art." He didn't seemed particularly excited, but he handed it over to Richard with a noticeable amount of respect. Bill Houston shared the guard's uncertainty about it.

Later, Bill Houston wanted to read it again. He borrowed it and kept it for a while after supper. It was just nice to have a document created by other prisoners. He couldn't make any sense of the poem, but sadness overcame him when he looked at it. He gave it back to Richard without comment.

But he thought about it off and on all night, and the next day without any preliminaries he said, "That's a beautiful poem, Richard. I'd like to take a copy with me on my ride."

Richard said nothing, but he jumped up and moved about his cell. "I'll think about it," he said finally.

Bill Houston and Richard talked a lot about what each was going to have for his final meal. Bill Houston wanted steak. Richard couldn't decide between chicken and pork. Bill Houston was grateful to know they wouldn't be eating the same thing. It seemed appropriate that the State of Arizona should provide them with a variety of foods before their big finish. Bill Houston didn't like to hear the guards calling it The Last Supper. It was a common prison expression, but he'd already heard enough about how Richard Clay Wilson would turn out to be his savior.

It was getting on his nerves. "I never asked you to die for me," he told Richard.

Richard only put his earphones over his head and pretended to be alone in the universe.

"C'mon, Richard." Bill Houston waved his hand before their window. "Hey. C'mon."

When Richard removed his earphones, tiny music came out of them like the whirring of a bug.

"Listen. How about reading me your poem one time?"

Richard appeared lost in a haze of considerations.

"Fact is, I read terrible, Richard. So that's why I'm asking you."

Richard opened the small stereo cassette box that housed the poem like a jewel. He unfolded the document and stepped back, standing himself up on the far side of his cell where Bill Houston could get a bigger picture of him. But he cast his gaze toward the corner, where there was nobody. "Talking Richard Wilson Blues," he said. "By Richard Clay Wilson." And he read in a Baptist sing-song:

> "I felt like a man of honor of substance,
>   but the situation was dancing underneath me—
>   once I walked into the living room at my sister's
>   and saw that the two of them, her and my sister,
>   had turned sometime behind my back not exactly
>   fatter, but heavy, or squalid, with cartoons
>   moving on the television in front of them,
>   surrounded by laundry, and a couple of Coca-Colas
>   standing up next to the iron on the board.

Angels

I stepped out into the yard of bricks
and trash and watched the light light
up the blood inside each leaf,
and I asked myself, Now what is the rpm
on this mother? Where do you turn it on?
I think you understand how I felt.

"I'm not saying everything changed in the space
of one second of seeing two women, but I did
start dragging her into the clubs with me. I insisted
she be sexy. I just wanted to live.
And I did: some nights were so sensory
I felt the starlight landing on my back
and I believed I could set fire to things with my fingers.
But the strategies of others broke my promise.
At closing time once, she kept talking to a man
when I was trying to catch her attention to leave.
It was a Negro man, and I thought of black limousines
and black masses and black hydrants filled
with black water. I thought I might smack her face, or spill
    a glass,
but instead I opened him up with my red fishing knife
and I took out his guts and I said, 'Here they are,
motherfucker, nigger, here they are.'
There were people frozen around us. The lights had just
    come on.
At that moment I saw her reading me and reading me
from the side of the room where I saw her standing,
the way the sacred light played across her face.

"Right down the middle from beginning to end
my life pours into one ocean, into this prison
with its empty ballfield and its empty
preparations. If she ever comes to visit me

to hell with her, I won't talk to her.
God kill you all. I'm sorry for nothing.
I'm just an alien from another planet.

"I am not happy. Disappointment
lights its stupid fire in my heart,
but two days a week I staff
the Max Security laundry above the world
on the seventh level, looking at two long roads
out there that go to a couple of towns.
Young girls accelerating through the intersection
make me want to live forever,
they make me think of the grand things,
of wars and extremely white, quiet light that never dies.
Sometimes I stand against the window for hours
tuned to every station at once, so loaded on crystal
meth I believe I'll drift out of my body.

"Jesus Christ, your doors close and open,
you touch the Maniac Drifters, the Fireaters,
I could say a million things about you
and never get that silence. That is what I mean
by darkness, the place where I kiss your mouth,
where nothing bad has happened.
I'm not anyone but I wish I could be told
when you will come to save us. I have written
several poems and several hymns, and one
has been performed on the religious
ultra-high-frequency station. And it goes like this."

Without waiting for any applause, Richard went immediately
back to his bunk and returned the poem to its case.

Foster, the elderly suppertime relief guard, had joined them
during Richard's recital of the poem. "Who's a maniac drifter?"

he asked now. Bill Houston was embarrassed. He thought it must be an insult to ask any questions about Richard's poem—Foster ran the risk of revealing that parts of it were stupid.

"That's a gang on the Southside," Richard said, "and the Fireaters, too. I was a friend to them. Once upon a time I carried a message. And then they had a war." He held up his head in his annoying way. "They in my poem," he said with genuine pride.

The three of them stood chained together by an awkward silence, and yet separated by prison bars. "I'm not supposed to tell you this," Foster said. And then he didn't tell them anything.

"Well?" Bill Houston said.

"They're not going to say anything till the last minute," Foster said. "But I know for a fucking-A fact that Richard's appeal went through this afternoon. My sister works over in the Court of Appeals. They're going to hang up the paper so you don't find out for a while—but I hate to see you sweat, Richard."

"I ain't sweating."

"What about my appeal?" Bill Houston felt his supper turning to stone inside him.

"Well, I just told you everything I know."

"Can't you find out for me? C'mon, Mr. Foster."

"I can't because it's Friday. If anything happens now, it'll be off-hours, and my sister wouldn't know about it anyway."

"Man—I ain't even been *worried.*" His legs went soft on him. "I need to get pre*pared.*" He sat on the bunk. He couldn't see Richard now, only Foster. "I need some reasons for this shit."

He felt the sympathy in their silence, but it was only silence.

"When you go up the pipe—does it hurt?" he asked Foster. "How does it feel?"

"I don't know. You tell me. Drop us a line, okay?" Even Bill Houston laughed at this, and he realized he was taking an attitude that made him look small. He should have been the one to say, "I'll drop you a line."

He resolved to be a better sport and show a cheerful disposition. Five AM Tuesday was the scheduled hour of his execution.

Did it ever cool off in this town? A downpour that morning had made a flood, but only three hours later no record of it lay anywhere on the hospital grounds, except for two puddles in the basins gouged out by children's feet beneath a pair of swings.

There were a sandbox and a push-me-go-round beside the swings, which were near the front gate. To see them made Jamie think for the first time that of course children must be housed here—children born crazy, and never sane in all their lives. If I'm a little out of it now, she thought, at least I can call up a few memories of the real days.

At the kiosk by the gate, she handed the guard her pass. "So! Three hours!" He fastened the pass to his clipboard and began studiously copying data from it onto his gate-list.

"I could be back a lot sooner. This is my first shot out of the box."

"I guessed that." He was an old man. "First time is always three hours." There was whiskey on his breath.

"I don't know if I can really handle it," Jamie said.

"You can handle it." He returned her pass and she signed his list. When she turned to go he said, "My pen."

"I was going to give it back to you. You think I'd steal your old pen?"

He gave an exaggerated shrug, his eyes glittering pinkly. You're happy now, you old drunk. But wait till you're watching The Movie Only You Can See.

Wait, she told herself; attitude. Attitude of Gratitude.

For the first time this summer, she stepped out onto the streets. Now she was grateful for her Welfare tennis shoes: a half-block west of her down Van Buren, three prostitutes loitered at a bus stop in festive dresses and bright stretch-pants and hip boots and spiked heels; but no one would mistake a goony little thing like herself for one of the day shift.

Before she could grow accustomed to the feel of pavement, her taxi arrived, a bright yellow Chevy. On the door she reached out and opened was stenciled: C.O.P.S.—Cabs On Patrol.

"Air conditioning!" she said.

"I wouldn't go near this cab if they didn't give me refrigeration," the driver said. He had a head of pitiful brown hair that reminded her of Bill Houston's, and it made her sad. "You're the one going to the Annex?" he said.

"You got it," she said.

Their route took them south and east, through the downtown, toward the freeway, and now she saw all the signs of the recent deluge—wet spots on the pavement, some oily pools in the gutters —she understood Phoenix had no sewers—and dark stains on the scaly hide of palm trees, beneath which lifeless brown fronds, some of them long as a man, had been scattered by the winds. The smog had washed out of the air, and as they rode the freeway, the flatness of the Southside to their right and the tall buildings of central Phoenix to their left looked beautifully varnished and free of imperfections.

This was the way she had hoped it would be—clean and clear.

Far to the east, she saw some mountains that she and Dwight Snow had spent some time watching one day, a day they'd seemed more like monsters. It was enough for them now to look like mountains.

. . .

"Wow. Kind of a no-man's-land out here, huh?" She counted her change carefully, and then got out of the cab and stood beside it.

"Probably someday, this whole desert is going to be a jail," the cabbie said. Jamie tipped him a dollar and he drove away.

The Maricopa County Jail Annex—out here in the middle of nothing, two or three miles from the Phoenix Sky Harbor—looked a little flimsy to Jamie, a little too chain-link and pre-fab to hold any person bent seriously on escape. The complex of structures was dominated by a long yellow building of a single storey that seemed just to peter out. They were still building it; it grew hideless and then skeletal and then collapsed into piles of unshaped materials at its far end, near a dirt exercise yard with a couple of basketball hoops standing around in it hopelessly.

She displayed her pass to the guard at the front gate, but he refused her entrance, directing her instead to the Visitors' Gate on the compound's other side, quite a ways down the road. "If I faint in this heat," she said, "please come rescue me."

The day was humid after the rain. Perspiration burned in her eye sockets and ran down out of her hair. She started to feel overwhelmed, walking by a prison compound through the searing moonscape beside the dry bed of the Salt River. A breeze brought the stench of the City of Phoenix Landfill down the empty river and wrapped it around her face.

The Visitors' Gate gave way to a tiny compound separated by chain-link and razor-barb from the jail proper, and occupied solely by a large sky-blue house trailer. The guard at the gate accepted her pass. But stepping through the archway beside his kiosk, she made the metal detector speak with crazed alarm.

She was afraid. "I gave you everything."

The guard appeared unruffled. He ran his hand-held detector up her left leg, over her head and down. it squeaked when it neared her teeshirt's breast pocket. "That a pack of smokes?"

"Yeah, but they ain't metal," she said.

"Even the tin foil in a cigaret pack sets it off. These are high-powered. Not like the airport." Jamie had never been in an airport.

He accepted the pack from her and added it to her coins and keys—keys to doors she would never confront again—in a small plastic tray. He placed her property in a locker inside his kiosk.

"You mean I can't take in my cigarets?"

"Sorry. Not in an open pack." Together they went up the brief walk and into the visitors' trailer.

Inside, the air was crisp, and her perspiration began to dry. The area was furnished like a lunchroom—vending machines, fluorescent lighting, plastic chairs, tables of indestructible blond false wood. She spent a good two minutes drinking from the humming grey water fountain, giving herself a headache. She was still standing beside it, breathing hard, when two guards escorted Burris through the trailer's opposite door. He was handcuffed. And it was obvious nobody liked him. It was the first thing she sensed from the three guards in the room.

But the guards retreated to opposite ends of the trailer, giving them a form of privacy. Burris sat across from her at one of the cafeteria-style tables. He was really happy to see her, that much was plain. "Hey—all right. Jamie," he said. "Welcome to the fort."

"Don't seem like much of a fort to me," she said. "If you just stared hard at that jailhouse it'd fall over."

Frowning and smiling, he raised his shackled hands and put a finger to his lips.

She laughed. "You don't look too rehabilitated with that scroungy beard all over your face. I liked it better when you were shaved."

She saw that in many ways he was her brother now. She loved him. But all she felt able to do was to kid around.

"That tobacco in your pouch there?" She indicated the pocket of his workshirt. "Think you can roll me a cigaret with your hands tied?"

"Yeah, it's tobacco. Wish it was something else." He managed to roll two cigarets without much difficulty, despite his handcuffs. Neither of them said a word during this operation. Jamie had to call one of the guards over for a light.

They both smoked. "Wish it was something else," he said again, laughing slyly.

"I got a little bent around by them chemicals," she told him.

"We had some high old times, didn't we?

"Yeah. But I mean, I'm serious. I was in the nuthouse. I'm still in the nuthouse."

"I know, Mom told me about it."

"So, I'm going in a whole nother direction now."

"Well, you look good. You look great."

"Oh yeah. I feel one hundred percent better," she said, "maybe more."

"You were just fucked up on drugs," Burris said.

"No. It was more. Much more," she said. "Over into the area of religion."

"No kidding," he said. "Like Mom."

"Like Mom," she said. "Exactly."

"Not like Jeanine I hope," Burris said.

"Not like Jeanine," Jamie assured him.

They smoked their cigarets. She tried to think of a few things to say. But she really didn't want to ask about the food.

She said, "I mean, sure, I was just fucked up on drugs. But it's kind of like you could look at it two ways."

"I was going nuts over dope, too," he said. "But I'm okay now."

"You all cleaned out?"

He looked sheepish. "Well, not exactly. There's a little something available in here every once in a while—you know."

"Well, I'm clean," she said. "I'm going to Narcotics Anonymous. I'll be in therapy, a halfway house, One Day at a Time, Attitude of Gratitude, the whole program. I mean to get my kids back, or die on the way."

"I can respect that, Jamie. It takes balls."

"I'm more scared than I ever been," she said frankly.

The door behind Jamie opened, and the guard brought in another visitor, a boy no older than Burris. Without thinking about it, Jamie felt their interview had reached an end.

"I got a note from Bill, is why I came. I came here with a message."

He grew visibly paler. His eyes were wet, and he was wordless.

"He says, 'Tell Burris he'll still be my brother.' "

He released his breath.

"They're fixing to kill him tomorrow, you know about that?" she said.

"Course I know," he said. "It's all I ever think about."

"I didn't know if they told you that kind of stuff, or what."

"They tell me. They want me to think about it."

"Well, if they really go ahead and do it to him—don't think he's on your conscience. He's past that. He's resentment-free. Nobody holds any of it against you, Burris." She wanted to give him peace. All she could think of to communicate it was to say, "Rest easy."

"Okay. I appreciate it, Jamie." And clearly he did.

Brian was having himself a great time, going over their heads with the clippers. "You just fucking with me," Richard told him. "I know my appeal gone through. Hold up!" he said, raising a hand. Brian stopped the clippers, and Richard sneezed violently.

"You're allergic to your own hair," Brian concluded.

Bill Houston sat on his bunk listening to this, running his hand around his new crew-cut. "This is humiliation," he said. "How much poison gas could stay in a little bit of hair? They don't really need to do this. Fuckers."

"It's cooler," Richard said. "My head feels cool."

"My head feels stupid," Bill Houston said.

"My appeal gone through anyway. They tell me tomorrow. Be a big surprise."

"I wouldn't know anything about that," Brian said.

"Maybe mine went through, too. Maybe they'll tell me tomorrow," Bill Houston said.

"Well, you got about eight more hours. Anything can happen," Brian said. "They'll crank things up in the middle of the night, if they have to—the whole Court of Appeals, everything."

"Eight more hours!"

"I'll be here. I had my shift changed around just for you," Brian said.

"I'm glad to have you," Bill Houston said sincerely. "You count as one of my friends. You're one of my friends, too, Richard."

"You won't have no friends in eight hours."

Bill Houston nodded—but nobody could see him nod; Brian was in Richard's cell. "There's always some kind of a countdown, though, ain't there? That's part of the whole story, ain't it?"

The clippers in the next cell ceased whirring. In the quiet moment, he couldn't even be sure who, if anyone, was there. He could never be connected: there was always something—bars, or laws, or words—in the way. It was only deep inside that he felt he made some contact. And then he couldn't be sure.

"Wash out your cup, Houston. Get it real clean."

He was startled. "What is it?" he said. He still couldn't see them.

"Man! This my favorite hotel!" This was Richard.

There was a terrible popping noise, and Bill Houston was up and hanging onto the bars.

Brian stepped over to his cell holding a big green bottle. "You're one of my friends, too, Mr. Houston." Champagne.

The Highway Patrol kept the prison side of Route 89 clear of the seekers and desirers, the ones who had to be there, the ones who sought to know. But the dirt margin of the road on the town side was lined with campers and motorcycles and trucks, with their owners and the children and families of the owners, who placed their forearms and elbows on these machines and leaned on them quietly for support during their vigil. It was dark. The blue roof-lights of the police raked their faces. Everything about the moment conspired to keep them silent: the death of stars in the east where the sun prepared to rise out of Tucson eighty miles away, the deep emptiness of the pre-dawn heavens, the imperious stupor of the Arizona State Prison Complex across the road and over the squad cars parked on its shoulder and beyond a cultivated field of cotton, its sand-colored structures on fire with the orange light of numberless sodium arc-lamps, and over all of the dawn of execution day, the desert night's dry foreboding, the negligent powerful breath of the day's coming heat, the heat that burns away each shadow and incinerates every last particle of shit inside the heart. But at this hour it was still cool—in their hands some of these people cradled styrofoam cups of steam.

The lawyer Fredericks was among them, and they troubled him. What made them think that after twenty years of merciless forbearance in dealing with murderers, the state would choose suddenly this morning to press its intentions to their end, and finish Bill Houston? Fredericks didn't feel like one of them. It seemed to him they represented mostly the very people who'd be incarcerated here tomorrow, goodtimers in sleeveless sweatshirts and teeshirts vulgarly inscribed ("The Itty Bitty Titty Committee")—slogans without meaning, transmissions into space— Honk If You Know Jesus and National Rifle Association bumper emblems nearly effaced by wind-driven sand—the children grubby and crew-cut, the women splayfooted and rubber-thonged —where were the young ladies apparelled for tennis, apparelled for golfing? Where were the outraged owners of the establishment? The bankers, the people with tie-pins and jeweled letter openers and profoundly lustrous desks of mahogany, the workers of all this machinery of law and circumstance? The people he couldn't fight—the people who were never here? The truth was, he knew, that they had enough to keep them occupied. They were busy, complete people. They didn't need to come here in the dark night to seek warmth around the fire of murder or draw close to the ceremonies of a semi-public death.

But these people around him—who'd probably gone to the same school as William Houston, Jr., or been acquainted with one or more of his relatives or had the same parole officer—came here because they sensed that why they themselves had not been executed was inexplicable, a miracle. And as best they could, they had to find out what it was like.

> *How does it feel.*
> *Tell me how does it feel.*
> *With no direction home.*
> *A complete unknown . . .*

But Fredericks didn't hear that song, except as it issued from their collective dream of suffocation. He heard only the radios playing a news program, an eye-witness show about this execution, broadcast from the west side of the prison, near the main entrance, where radio and TV news teams had been parked since suppertime last night. What made them all believe it would actually happen? What hadn't he been told? I am here in my white dress shirt and brown loafers. Someone is keeping a secret. I am the little boy whose dog is dead.

Cars had ceased arriving. The light in the east was blue-grey. People were talking a bit louder now; there was laughter; they were nervous. The children were getting anxious, quarreling and chasing aimlessly around all the cars, eluding their mothers.

Fredericks determined in his mind not to look at his watch. After a minute, he had to take off his watch and put it in his pocket to keep from glancing at its face. And then he went over to his Volvo and threw the watch onto the front seat and walked away from it. He just wanted to find out if he would know, without a watch, when it was time.

It was time.

Brian said, "Mr. Houston? Let's take you for a ride up that pipe."

He couldn't believe he'd actually been asleep. All night he had lain with the Unmade, with God, the incredible darkness, the huge blue mouth of love.

I'm going to be turned into space. This is the hour of my death.

He couldn't stand. "Didn't the appeal go through?"

"No," Brian said.

"Well it doesn't even have to go through. They just have to get it started."

"Nothing happened. This is it, Bill."

"See you, Richard."

"See you," Richard's voice said.

"Are they all in there?"

"Everybody's in there but you and me," Brian said.

He stood up. He had a desire out of nowhere to let everyone know it was all right; everything was fine.

"Take off your pants," Brian said in a kindly way.

"Take off my pants?"

He looked down at his prison-issue jeans. What did everybody want his pants for? He thought he was going to cry.

"We can't have a big pile of clothes all soaked with gas," Brian said. "Didn't anybody tell you?"

"You mean I got to be naked?" Tears sprang out of his eyes. It must have been years since he'd cried tears before another; but this was too much. They hadn't warned him about this.

"You can keep your shorts on," Brian said.

He stood there handcuffed, shorn nearly bald, wearing only his white underpants. It was chilly and he was shaking, but it wasn't important, even if they thought he was afraid. Two guards from CB-6 were present, and he noticed them. Familiar faces. He nodded. There was a young doctor from the clinic standing there, and a short gentleman reading out loud. The warden. The Order of Execution. The door was open. There was a hearse parked outside it in the early morning. Only one.

The witnesses were already behind the glass. He couldn't hear, and shook his head. Was everything behind glass?

The warden stopped reading. "Is something wrong?"

Wrong? He stood next to Brian facing the warden, the doctor, the two guards. Every one of them was terrified. They were all scared to death of what was happening. The warden's voice trembled. "Do you have anything to say at this time?" he asked Bill Houston.

Bill Houston was floored by the question. "Is there something I'm supposed to say now?"

Everyone was confused.

Brian said suddenly, "I want you to know I don't think you deserve to die. I think you been healed."

Nobody knew how to react. They all looked around. It was obvious even the warden didn't know if Brian had just broken a rule. "I really feel that way," Brian said defiantly.

"Thank you," Bill Houston said.

They all stood there in a long silence. What was going on now?

"What's going on?" Bill Houston asked.

The warden looked green and ill. "We still have a couple of minutes," he said. "I think we should wait, don't you?" He glanced around helplessly.

Bill Houston whispered to Brian, "I don't think I can stand up any more."

Taking him by the elbow, Brian helped Bill Houston into the gas chamber.

A truth filled up the chamber: there was nothing left for him now. The door had shut on his life. It said DEATH IS THE MOTHER OF BEAUTY. He couldn't hear a thing. He wondered if they'd put cotton in his ears.

And then there was a faint rattling in the pipe to his right, and the sound of boiling liquid beneath him. He looked down at the length of surgical tubing that ran from his chest to the door. There it goes. Up that tube. Boom boom boom boom boom boom boom. That's all that's ever really been important. A visible vapor was curling up over his knees.

He held his breath. Every rivet of metal was a jewel to him. He felt he could hold his breath forever—no problem. Boom, boom. Even as his heart accelerated, it seemed to him inexplicably that his heart was slowing down. You can get right in between each beat, and let the next one wash over you like the best and biggest warm ocean there ever was. His eyes were on fire. He hated to shut them, but they hurt. He wanted to *see*. Boom! Was there ever anything as pretty as that one? Another coming . . . boom! Beautiful! They just don't come any better than that.

He was in the middle of taking the last breath of his life before he realized he was taking it. But it was all right. Boom! Unbelievable! And *another* coming? How many of these things do you mean to give away? He got right in the dark between heartbeats, and rested there. And then he saw that another one wasn't going to come. That's it. That's the last. He looked at the dark. I would like to take this opportunity, he said, to pray for another human being.

Casablanca Cafe, normally closed before six AM, was open early for the execution. Fredericks looked in through the window, and saw that the place was still empty. The crowd was still down by the highway. At this moment they would all be looking toward the Death House, watching the rust-colored pipe that rose ostentatiously above the little building that was itself obscured by other prison buildings; and as the chamber beneath it was voided by a suction pump, some would believe they smelled the stench of rarefied cyanous vapors, like peach blossoms. And they would be excruciated, amused, reassured, or made pensive, depending on who they were.

"Everybody's still over by the show," the waitress said. Her name was Clair. Fredericks knew her name, but that was all.

"Was it on the radio?" Fredericks asked her.

"Just now. It'll be on again in two minutes, I guarantee you."

"Can I have some Scotch in my coffee?"

Clair brought him a pot of coffee, a fifth of Black Label, and a white cup. In a few minutes, as they listened to the radio that sat beside the cash register, the morning produced its soft light. William H. Houston, Jr., had been put to death. Richard Clay Wilson's sentence had been commuted to life.

"A lot of people got finessed this morning," Fredericks told Clair.

Clair stood by the window, holding aside its curtain delicately between two fingers and watching the street. "Us, too," she told him now. "Everybody's just zooming right out of town. The only ones who made a profit on this deal was Seven-Eleven. They sold everybody coffee."

"And you sold me Scotch," Fredericks said.

"Oh, call it a gift, okay? We don't have a license."

Fredericks stayed a long time in Casablanca Cafe. For a while he napped in the booth, his head thrown back, his mouth open, and he woke feeling furry inside and disoriented.

As he was paying for his coffee, at the instant he was putting one of the free toothpicks into his mouth, he sensed the presence of someone nearby, staring at him. The mood was palpable and real, but he knew there was hardly anyone in the place, just a man reading a magazine, which he held flat on the table beside his bowl of soup. Fredericks looked around a minute before he saw the portrait of Elvis Presley on the wall behind the cash register, almost directly in front of him. Rendered in iridescent paint on black velvet, hovering before a brilliant microphone, the face of the dead idol seemed on the brink of speech.

Fredericks stepped out into the terrible noon and stood by the road with his hands in his pockets, his face shaded by the brim of a straw hat, and chewed his toothpick, aware that he looked very much like a country lawyer. He was still young, and it was completely possible that soon he'd begin carrying out his original intention of getting himself elected to something or other. But the truth was, he knew, that he'd been irretrievably sidetracked right at the start by his stint as a public defender, and that he'd probably continue the rest of his life as a criminal lawyer because, in all honesty, there was a part of him that wanted to help murderers go free.

Most of his clients ended up in Florence. He'd spent a lot of time here. And he would be here a great deal more, in this town of bored dirt consisting mainly of a prison shimmering at this moment in waves of heat, a town that was always quiet except for the sounds of wind coming across the desert and ropes banging against flagpoles—where every evening the iridescent-on-velvet face of Elvis Presley climbed the twilight to address all the bankrupt cafes.

It was Fredericks's understanding that the prisoners had a story: that each night for months, at nine precisely, a light had burned in a window in the town, where the men on one cellblock's upper tier could see it and wonder, and imagine, each one, that it shone for him alone. But that was just a story, something that people will tell themselves, something to pass the time it takes for the violence inside a man to wear him away, or to be consumed itself, depending on who is the candle and who is the light.

A Note on the Type

The text of this book was set in Electra, a type face designed by William Addison Dwiggins (1880–1956) for the Mergenthaler Linotype Company and first made available in 1935. Electra cannot be classified as either "modern" or "old style." It is not based on any historical model, and hence does not echo any particular period or style of type design. It avoids the extreme contrast between thick and thin elements that marks most modern faces, and it is without eccentricities that catch the eye and interfere with reading. In general, Electra is a simple, readable type face that attempts to give a feeling of fluidity, power, and speed.

Composed, printed, and bound by The Haddon Craftsmen, Inc., Scranton, Pennsylvania

Designed by Sara Reynolds

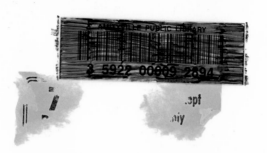
1

Johnson, Denis
    Angels